PRAISE FOR *THE CONCH BEARER*

★ "Divakaruni keeps her tale fresh and riveting with details of India's sights, smells, and tastes, with characters that possess both good and evil, and with her exploration of the fine line between faith and magic. Young readers can only hope for more from this master storyteller."
—*Publishers Weekly*, starred review

★ "With so many fantasies being published, what's special about this one? It's the unique setting, along with the elegance of Divakaruni's writing. The slums of 'Kalcutta' are so richly created that readers can almost smell them. . . . This speaks directly to children, in a very enticing voice."
—*Booklist*, starred review

"This quest adventure has an exotic flavor. . . . Readers can sympathize with [Anand's] struggle and long for his success. This traditional story in fresh new clothing should appeal to middle-grade readers."
—*School Library Journal*

"The rich details in the story . . . offer readers a colorful snapshot of [India's] land and its culture."
—*Houston Chronicle*

The CONCH BEARER

CHITRA BANERJEE DIVAKARUNI

ALADDIN PAPERBACKS
NEW YORK   LONDON   TORONTO   SYDNEY

ALADDIN PAPERBACKS
An imprint of Simon & Schuster Children's Publishing Division
1230 Avenue of the Americas, New York, NY 10020
Copyright © 2003 by Chitra Banerjee Divakaruni
All rights reserved, including the right of
reproduction in whole or in part in any form.
ALADDIN PAPERBACKS and colophon are registered trademarks
of Simon & Schuster, Inc.
First published in the United States by Roaring Brook Press, a
division of Holtzbrinck Publishing Holdings Limited Partnership, 2003
Designed by Jennifer Browne
Manufactured in the United States of America
First Aladdin Paperbacks edition March 2005
2 4 6 8 10 9 7 5 3 1
The Library of Congress has cataloged the hardcover edition
as follows:
Divakaruni, Chitra Banerjee, 1956–
The conch bearer / Chitra Banerjee Divakaruni. — 1st ed.
p. cm.
"A Neal Porter Book."
Summary: In India, a healer invites twelve-year-old Anand to join
him on a quest to return a magical conch to its safe and rightful
home, high in the Himalayan mountains.
[1. Healers—Fiction. 2. Shells—Fiction. 3. Magic—Fiction.
4. Voyages and travels—Fiction. 5. India—Fiction.] I. Title.
PZ7.D6295Co 2003
[Fic]—dc21   2003008578
ISBN 0-689-87242-9 (Aladdin pbk.)

Once more for my three men,

Abhay,

Anand,

Murthy

My deepest thanks to

Sandra Dijkstra, superb agent

Neal Porter, delightful editor

Murthy, Anand, Abhay, my inspirations

Tatini Banerjee and Sita Divakaruni, my cheering team

Baba Muktananda, Swami Chinmayananda, and

Gurumayi, my guides

A STRANGE OLD MAN

Anand shivered as he carried a heavy load of dirty dishes from the tea stall to the roadside tap for washing. It was cold today, colder than he ever remembered it being in the city of Kolkata, and all he had on was his threadbare green shirt. It was windy, too; a bitter, biting wind with a strange, burning smell to it, as though something big, like a lorry or a petrol truck, had exploded on a nearby street. But nothing like that had happened. Anand would have heard if it had, because gossip traveled fast here, on the narrow, congested alleys of Bowbajar Market. So maybe, Anand thought with a grin, it was just his boss, Haru, the tea stall's owner, frying onion pakoras once again in stale peanut oil!

The grin transformed Anand's face, turning him from a solemn, gangly twelve-year-old with knobby knees and elbows into the happy young boy he'd been before ill luck had turned his life upside down two years ago. For a moment, his black eyes sparkled with merry, mischievous intelligence—but then the grin faded, replaced by the cautious expression he had learned since he started working for Haru.

With a sigh, Anand pushed back the shock of untidy hair that kept falling into his eyes because he couldn't afford a haircut. Then he got back to scrubbing the huge aluminum pot in which Haru had boiled milk-tea all day yesterday. There were stubborn black scorch marks all along the bottom, and if he didn't manage to get them out, Haru would be sure to yell at him and cuff him on the ear. But it was hard to get anything clean, Anand thought, brushing his hair impatiently away from his eyes again, when the only thing he was given to scrub with was the ash from the tea stall's coal fire, which left his fingers red and itchy. The one time he had asked for dishwashing soap, it had earned him a slap and a curse from Haru.

"Dishwashing soap!" added Haru, shouting so that everyone within fifty yards could hear him. "For fifty years we've been using ash to clean the tea stall's pots, but now it's not good enough for Prince Anand! And who's going to pay for the soap? Your dad, the millionaire?"

The customers sitting on rickety chairs around the stall had sniggered, and Anand had ducked into a dark corner of the storage area, blinking away furious tears. That bit about his father had hurt more than the slap. He hadn't seen his father, whom he loved more than anyone in the world—except possibly his mother and his younger sister, Meera—for two years now. That was when his father had left for Dubai. He had left unwillingly—but he had no choice.

"The job this company is offering me is too good to turn down," he told Anand, who was ten years old at the time. "Business is bad in Kolkata right now . . . I've been out of work for months, and we've spent almost all our savings."

He explained to Anand that Dubai was a city on another continent, so far away that you could get to it only by flying in a plane for hours and hours. He was going to work as a construction-site overseer there, building houses for the rich with huge iron gates and marble fountains in the courtyards. He would make a lot of money, and he would send most of it back to his family every month. He hoped to save up enough money in two years—three at the most—so that he'd never have to go this far from his family again.

Anand's father had sent a money order that first month, just as he had promised, and they had had a great feast at home, with much laughter and joking. His mother had cooked lamb, their father's favorite dish, and had wiped at her eyes with the corner of her sari when she thought the children were not looking. She had opened a savings account with half of the money, just as they had planned. The following month, and the next, she had put away half the money—and still there had been enough to buy Meera a doll with real hair that you could comb. For

Anand, she had bought a book—because books were what he liked the most. It was titled *Persian Fairy Tales*. He had spent many blissful hours reading about a magic apple that could cure you of any disease if you smelled it once, and a telescope that could show you anything in the world that you wanted to see.

But after a few months, the money orders had stopped unaccountably. There were no letters, either. Worried, Anand's mother wrote letter after letter to his father, but no reply came. Finally, they had to give up the pretty flat they lived in, with tubs of jasmine on a little balcony that looked out on a park, and move into the one-room shack in the slum area that was their home now. Anand's mother had to take up a job as a cook in a rich household. It had been enough to allow them to limp along—until the terrible thing that happened to Meera. Mother had used up all her savings taking Meera to doctor after doctor. But none of the doctors had been able to cure her.

As he stacked the washed pots and tea glasses on the counter, Anand wished—as he had done many times secretly in the past year—that someone would give him a magic apple like the one he had read about. And a magic telescope.

Once, he had confided in his mother about his secret wish.

"Then I could make Meera better, and we could see where father was, and if he was all right," he'd said.

His mother had sighed. "Those things happen only in storybooks, son. Don't you know that by now?"

Anand had nodded, feeling foolish. He didn't tell her that, deep down inside, he believed that magic could happen. No, that it *did* happen. That it was happening all the time, all around them, except that most people didn't know about it. Sometimes he could almost sense it whizzing by him, rapid as an invisible hummingbird. If only he could figure out how to grab it and make it carry him along, too, his entire life would change. He was sure of it.

"You! Boy!" Haru shouted from the front counter. "It's time to take the cloth merchant his morning tea. Can't you remember anything without me having to tell it to you over and over?"

Anand jumped up and poured four steaming glasses of tea for the cloth merchant and his assistants. He placed them in a wire carrier and wrapped a large helping of onion pakoras in a newspaper. Then he ran to the next street where the fabric shop was, careful to avoid potholes so the tea would not spill. Shaheen, the cloth merchant, liked his tea hot, and his glass filled to the brim. The smell of the hot pakoras he was carrying was driving Anand crazy. He was so hungry! He had to clench his teeth hard to resist the urge to sneak a pakora—just one—into his mouth. He hoped that Shaheen was having a good day, because then he might reward Anand with a tip of twenty-five or even fifty paise. But today Shaheen was busy with a customer and merely nodded when Anand brought the tea.

Anand walked back, disappointed, trying to block the little voice inside his head that jeered at him for not eating that pakora when he had the chance. His break, when he was allowed to have a few minutes' rest, a cup of tea, and maybe a plate of stale food from the previous day, wasn't going to be for hours. How cold it was! The chill pressed down on him like an icy hand. He should have worn his shawl over his shirt. But he'd left it behind for Meera—she'd been coughing, and it was so damp in their shack.

He found himself wondering once more what could have gone wrong with his father, that tall, handsome, laughing man who used to take Meera and him to see movies and buy them hot roasted peanuts. Had he been injured on the job, or even—Anand hesitated over the frightening word—killed? Or had he (and this was worse) decided to forget them?

He had overheard a neighbor lady talking to his mother about that once, when they were still living in the flat.

"Sometimes men go to a new country and come across another woman, a younger, prettier one. It's tempting for them to start a new life with her, to cut off ties—"

"My husband's not like that." Anand's mother spoke calmly enough, but her nostrils flared with anger. She stood up to indicate the conversation was over, and showed the neighbor out. Only Anand had seen the terrible doubt that had moved across her face like a rain cloud as she latched the door.

༼ ͡°͜ ͡° ༽

Deep in his troubled thoughts, Anand almost bumped into a group of children who were standing at the corner, waiting for the school bus. He tried not to stare hungrily at their neat, starched uniforms and polished shoes, and the casual way they swung their brightly colored satchels. But he couldn't help it. He wanted so much to be like them—and knew so well that it was out of his reach.

As he passed them, one of the boys pointed at him and whispered something to the girl standing next to him. She wrinkled her nose—*as though I were a bad smell*, Anand thought—and then they both burst out laughing. Anand's ears burned. They were laughing at him—at his dirty shirt with a button missing and his frayed pants and his too-long hair. He felt a sting of shame, and then anger. No, it was envy he felt. Because if there was one other thing he longed for, it was to be able to go to school again.

He remembered the day, almost a year earlier, when he'd awakened to the sound of his mother sobbing. This was unusual because she rarely wept. His heart sinking, he'd walked across the floor of the shack to where she sat with her head in her hands on her sleeping mat—they'd sold what little furniture they'd possessed by then—and even before she'd said a word, he'd known what was coming. She didn't have the money for the children's school fees any more.

Meera, being younger, had not minded much. She had thought it was kind of fun to be able to stay home and play all day. But Anand still remembered the pain he felt as he put his beloved books away in a corner. (They'd have to sell them back to Sengupta's Used Books a few months later.) He folded away his school uniforms—the two pairs of white shorts and the blue shirts with the logo that said HINDU BOYS ACADEMY embroidered on their pockets—which he took such pride in, washing them himself every day to make sure they were spotless. (Those, too, would have to be sold). But he was careful not to let his mother see how unhappy he was. She had so many troubles already. He didn't want to add to them. He had put on a pair of stained old khaki pants and his checkered shirt that was too tight under the arms and trudged over to Haru's tea stall. He'd overheard a neighbor who lived down the street say that Haru was looking for a boy to help him because the one who'd been working for him had run away.

"And no wonder!" the neighbor had added, cackling cruelly.

Anand soon learned what he meant. But he also knew he was lucky to find a job at all. Times were bad, and many grown men had no work. They were forced to beg on street corners—or worse, to turn to thievery and violence. Anand hated Haru's blistering tongue and ever-ready fists.

But when things got really bad, he would think about the look on his mother's face at the end of each week when he ran home and gave her whatever he had earned.

"My dear, good boy!" she'd say as she hugged him, a rare smile lighting up her face and making her seem years younger. "I couldn't have managed without your help! I'm so lucky to have a son like you."

Briefly, he would be happy. Briefly, it would make up for the things he'd lost. But it didn't make it easy to face the rest of the week—especially moments like this one.

With the children's laughter echoing in his ears, he closed his eyes tightly and clenched his fists. *I want my life to change*, he said fiercely inside his head, holding his breath until he grew dizzy, putting all his strength into the wish and launching it from him the way an archer sends forth an arrow. He could feel it speed across the sky, hot and bright, until it connected with something—or some-one. The sense of contact was so strong that Anand's body jerked backward from the impact. He opened his eyes, expecting to see this *something*. He didn't know what shape it would take, but surely it would be wondrous and radiant and magical. But all that lay in front of him was the famil-iar stretch of dirty pavement with rotting garbage piled along the gutter.

"You, boy!" Haru shouted as soon as he caught sight of Anand. "What took you so long? Loafing on the street corner, were you? I should give you a whack on your head. Can't you see there's customers waiting?"

Anand hurried over to the tables to ask people what they wanted to have. Most ordered only tea. A couple of clerks on their way to the office ordered sweets to take with them. Two college students—a young man and his girlfriend, Anand guessed—asked for a plate of pooris and alu dum. Anand's stomach growled, embarrassing him terribly, as he brought over the puffed fried bread and spicy potatoes, and the young woman gave him a curious look.

That was when he noticed the old man.

At first Anand thought that perhaps he was a beggar. He stood at the entrance of the tea stall, wrapped in a dirty white cotton shawl and carrying a walking stick made of cheap bamboo. A ragged cloth bag hung from his shoulder. He had matted gray hair and a straggly beard, and even on this cold day, his feet were bare. But unlike other beggars, he didn't gaze longingily at the glass cases filled with sweets. Instead—but surely Anand was mistaken— he seemed to be staring at Anand.

Haru, too, had noticed the old man.

"You there," he yelled. "What do you want? And, more importantly, do you have the money for it?" The old man said nothing. "I didn't think so!" Haru said, his mouth twisting. "In that case, get out of the way of my paying customers."

The man stood there as though he hadn't even heard

Haru, and for a moment Anand wondered if he was a bit soft in the head, like Meera had become after what had happened to her. He felt a stab of sympathy for him.

"Out! Out!" Haru yelled more loudly. "Do you think I've opened a poorhouse here? Useless beggar! Boy, kick him out of the stall!"

Anand went over to the old man and took him gently by the arm. How light his arm felt, as though he had feathers instead of bones! He was surprised by how warm the man's arm was. He'd expected the old man to be shivering, like himself, standing as he was in the wind, which was stronger now, swirling dust and torn newspapers along the street.

"Come on, grandfather," he said gently, "you'd better go home before he insults you further."

The old man did not protest. He followed docilely enough as Anand led him to the street corner. Did he even *have* a home? Anand wondered. He was surprised at how concerned he felt about leaving the old man by himself. It was almost as though he were abandoning him. Which was ridiculous, considering that Anand hadn't even set eyes on him until a few minutes earlier.

Just as Anand let go of his arm, the old man looked at him. His eyes were . . . blue? green? shimmery brown like the eyes of a tiger? Anand couldn't tell. He knew only that something tingled through him like an electric current when the old man looked at him.

"Wait here," Anand said impulsively. Then he ran back to the stall.

"Can I please take my tea break a little early today?" he asked Haru, in the small, scared voice the stall owner liked him to use.

Haru frowned. "What's the matter?" he said nastily. "Your mother didn't give you any breakfast?"

Anand swallowed his anger and stood with his head lowered.

"I guess you can go," Haru finally said, grumpily. "Seeing as there are no customers right now. But be sure to be back in ten minutes—or I'll cut your pay."

Anand nodded, poured himself a glass of tea, wrapped a few stale pooris in a torn newspaper, and left before Haru changed his mind.

He was afraid that the old man might have wandered off. But no, he was waiting exactly where Anand had left him. He seemed not to have moved at all—as though he were a statue. Or perhaps he just didn't have any place to go, Anand thought with a little catch in his heart.

"Here," he said with a smile, handing the man the tea and slipping the pooris into the bag he was carrying. "Drink this. It's nice and hot, and it'll make you feel better. Mean as he is, Haru does make a good cup of tea. You can eat the pooris later." He took the man's hand and closed his fingers around the glass. "I don't mean to rush you, but I've got only a few minutes. Then I have to go back, or Haru really will cut my pay. And I just can't afford that."

The old man raised the glass in a strong smooth motion that surprised Anand and drank till it was empty.

"You gave me your own food and drink," he said. "For that I thank you." His voice was deep and gravelly, as though it came from the bottom of the river, and he spoke the Bengali words with a slight accent, as though he had come from elsewhere. He made a small sign in the air above Anand's head, a gesture the boy had never seen before. Then he turned and, moving unexpectedly fast, disappeared around a corner.

Anand walked back to the stall musing. *Mother was right*, he thought. *Sharing what you have with others really makes you feel good.* What else could account for the warmth that suddenly flooded him, or the fact that he wasn't hungry at all, although—as Haru had guessed—there hadn't been anything to eat at home that morning.

THE NIGHT VISITOR

It was dark by the time Anand got off work, and he was very angry. Haru was supposed to let him go by 4 P.M., but he often found an excuse to keep Anand longer. Today he had claimed that Anand had not wiped the tables properly and made him do them all over again.

Anand had scrubbed the pocked wood of the tables furiously, biting his lip to make himself stay silent. Arguing, he knew, would only earn him a slap. Now he was going to be late for the market! Today was payday, and he had promised his mother that he would stop at the vegetable bazaar. For days now they'd had nothing to eat except potatoes and white radish boiled with rice, and he was tired of it. He had hoped to get a bunch of fresh, crisp spinach, or some sheem beans to fry up with chilies. But by now most of the pavement vendors would be gone. *If only I had the power to run my hands over the tables and make them new and shiny!* he thought. *But no, if I knew how to work that kind of changing magic, I'd start with Haru's black heart.*

Bone tired though he was, Anand ran all the way to the

vegetable market. Just as he had feared, the bazaar was deserted, the ground littered with wilted cabbage leaves and banana peels. Only the big stall with the neon lights, the one that charged extra for everything and had a big red sign that said NO BARGAINING, was still open. Anand walked up to it warily, knowing that most of the items there were beyond his budget. But maybe there would be something not so fresh. Then his eyes were caught by the pile of mangoes. Mangoes in winter! Where had the storekeeper found them? They were plump and soft and just the right ripeness, their skins a glowing orange streaked with red. How long had it been since Anand had eaten a mango? He swallowed, imagining the sweet juice that would fill his mouth when he took a big bite, and asked how much they were.

"Two rupees each," said the storekeeper in a bored voice. Obviously, he didn't think the ragged boy standing in front of him could afford the price.

Anand opened his mouth to protest. Why, the storekeeper was charging twice as much as what the pavement vendors would have charged! But he said nothing. The man would only shrug insolently and tell him to go elsewhere. He hesitated, then took out the meager bundle of rupee notes he had tucked into his waistband and peeled off two of them. He carefully picked the biggest, fattest mango, hefting it in his palm. Wouldn't Meera be amazed when he showed up with this beauty!

By now it was late and windier than ever, and Anand had to keep his head lowered to avoid the dust and debris flying through the air. Thankfully, he didn't feel cold. Why, he thought in surprise, he hadn't felt cold all day, not since he gave the old man his tea! He hoped the old man had found a place to shelter himself for the night. It looked like it was going to be a rough one.

The streets were strangely empty as Anand made his way home. Was it because it was dinnertime, or was it this unpleasant wind? The small businesses that lined the street—the printing presses and machine shops—had turned off their lights, padlocked their gates, and sent their employees home. With a brief pang of envy, Anand imagined them safe in their warm, lighted houses, listening to songs on the radio or sitting around a table, eating a hot meal, maybe a chicken curry with rice. After dinner the children would crowd around their father, begging for a story. The mother would bring bowls of sweet milk pudding from the kitchen. That was how it had been with his family, too, before . . . .

Anand shook his head to clear the memories. What use was it to long for what was no longer there? He'd better concentrate on getting home quickly. He'd have to start the cooking because Mother wouldn't be home until much later, and Meera couldn't be trusted to light the kerosene stove on her own. She couldn't do much of anything since the *bad-luck accident*, that's how he thought of it, had happened to her. He hoped she had remembered to wash the plates and fill the big earthen pitcher with water from the tenement's tube well. Sometimes when he came home, she would still be sitting on her bedding with a vacant look on her face, and he knew she hadn't moved from there since morning. But he never had the heart to scold her.

He passed the cigarette shop, surprised to see that it, too, was closed. Before today, no matter how late he had been in coming back from work, it had always been open, its shiny radio blaring hits from the latest Hindi movies. There was always a crowd of young men around it, joking and jostling around, smoking beedis or chewing on betel leaves and spitting out the red juice wherever they pleased. But today, with its shutters pulled down and locked, the shop looked abandoned and eerie, and Anand walked past it as quickly as he could.

Right around then he became aware that someone was following him. He wasn't sure how he knew it. There were no sounds—not that he would have heard footsteps in all this wind. Nor was there anyone behind him when he forced himself to whirl around and look. The street was empty and dark—a streetlight had burned out—and Anand realized that he was at the same crossing where Meera had been when the accident that had turned her strange and silent had occurred. He pushed the thought away from him with a shiver and quickened his steps. *There's no one behind me, no one*, he said to himself over and over, and, under that, *Mustn't fall, mustn't fall.* Because then, whatever was behind him would catch up.

There's no one behind me. Mustn't fall.

He was running now. There was a fog all around him, obscuring the shapes of the shacks and turning the alleys into unfamiliar, yawning tunnels. His foot caught on something, and he went sprawling. The mango fell from his hand and rolled into the darkness. Oh no! Not the mango he'd spent two whole hard-earned rupees on! He scrabbled desperately for it, but felt nothing but asphalt and dirt. He wanted to search more, but something told him it wasn't safe to delay any longer. Where had the fog come from, anyway? How could it be windy and foggy at the same time? Was this his street? Where was his house, then? He looked around wildly, not recognizing anything. *Help me!* He called inside his head, not knowing to whom he called. *Help!* He was ashamed to be acting this way, like a child. The fog in front of him thinned for a moment. Ah! There was his shack with its warped tin door! He had never been so happy to see it. He knocked frantically on the door, calling to Meera to open up, hurry, hurry. He heard her unsteady steps, then the bolt sliding across. He threw himself inside, slammed the door behind him, and bolted it again. He leaned his back against the door, his heart pounding. Meera stared at him, a startled look on her face.

He forced himself to smile because he didn't want to scare her. "Don't worry, Meera," he said, though his throat was so dry he could barely speak. "Everything's all right."

Then he heard the knocking. *Tap, tap, tong.* Someone was hitting the door with . . . a stick? a piece of metal? He could feel the vibration against his shoulder blades. He jumped away from the door and looked around for a weapon, something with which to defend himself and his sister. In the flickering light of the small oil lamp, he could see nothing except an old bonti, its blade dulled from years of cutting vegetables. Somehow he didn't think it would stop whoever was outside.

Then he heard the voice, deep and rusty, as if it had been at the bottom of a river for a long time.

"Anand," it said. "Let me in."

Anand didn't know how long he stood in the middle of the room, eyes squinched shut, heart pounding madly. But the knocking didn't stop, as he had hoped. There it was again.

Tap, tap, tong.

"Go away," he whispered through dry lips.

"Let me in, Anand," the voice said. "I won't hurt you."

Right! Anand thought. That's what all the evil beings in his storybooks said, the monsters and witches, the dakinis who drank blood.

"I don't believe you! I don't even know who you are!" he shouted. "Go away now, before I yell for the neighbors."

"Your neighbors won't come. They won't even hear

you over the wind. And even if they did, they'd be too scared, because of the killing—"

"How did you know about the . . . killing?" Anand asked, astonished, stumbling over the word. No one in the neighborhood spoke of it, not out loud like this, anyway. Like Anand, they all called it "the accident," as though renaming it could make it into something less dangerous.

The voice didn't answer his question. "In any case, you do know who I am," it said instead with a little laugh. "I'm the old man to whom you gave your tea."

Perhaps it was the laugh, or the memory of the old man's hand, light as a bird's foot in his hand, but Anand felt less scared. He wasn't completely convinced, though.

"Why did you follow me home?" he asked.

"Don't you know? You called for me—for us—and we came."

"I never called anyone," Anand said. Then he added, suspiciously, "What do you want from me?"

"Did you not call for help a little while ago?" the old man said.

"But that was in my head—"

"Exactly," said the man, a smile in his voice. "But you're right. I do want something. And in return I have something to offer you. But I can't discuss these things with a closed door between us. Please?"

Wondering if he was making a terrible mistake, Anand motioned to Meera to get behind him. *What if it's a trick?*

a voice inside him whispered. Ignoring it, he raised a trembling hand and unbolted the door. It was only when the door had creaked open on its hinges that he remembered that the man had said "*we* came."

But thank heavens, the old man was alone. Perhaps I misheard him, Anand thought. Something about him was different, though. Was it Anand's imagination, or did he seem straighter and taller? His white hair and beard glowed eerily in the dim light from the lamp as he stepped into the room, and there was a brightness in his eyes. The cloth bag was slung over his shoulder.

"Thank you," he said with a slight bow. "The wind was becoming rather unpleasant." As Anand watched, he walked to each corner of the room and made the same strange motion with his hand that Anand had seen him make earlier. Then he sat down on the mat the boy had spread out for him.

"It's very unusual for it to be so windy here," Anand said, mostly because he didn't know what else to say. He wondered if it had been the old man whom he had felt following him earlier. Somehow he didn't think so. The old man was strange, but Anand didn't feel scared when he looked at him. If anything, he felt happy. That was odd. Why should he feel happy looking at this ragged stranger whom he'd never met before today?

"I'm afraid I'm partly responsible for the wind," the old man was saying with a rueful grin.

"What do you mean? Did you . . . make . . . the wind happen?" As soon as he said it, Anand felt stupid. People didn't make winds happen.

But the old man didn't seem to think it was a stupid question. "I didn't," he replied. "Someone who wanted to stop me did. But before I explain things, is it possible to get a bite to eat? I'm starving. Only had a glass of tea all day, you know, and a few pooris!"

Anand jumped to his feet, embarrassed. "Of course! I'll start the rice and lentil stew right away. That's all we have, I'm afraid." He hunted around in the corner for the pot. Thankfully Meera had remembered to wash it today. He glanced at Meera, who was unusually quiet. She had crept close to the old man as he talked and was watching him intently. This surprised him. Ever since the killing, she'd been terrified of strangers, and on the few occasions when they had neighbors visiting them, she had curled up on her pallet in the far corner of the room, with the bed-clothes drawn over her head.

Anand lit the stove, threw a few handfuls of rice and lentils into the pot, and added water, salt, turmeric, and chili powder. In twenty minutes, it would form a bubbly stew. Once again, he wished he'd been able to pick up a few vegetables. And that mango! If he hadn't dropped it, he could have cut each of them a slice to eat after dinner. He wanted to kick himself for being so clumsy.

The lamp in the corner flickered and the flame grew

small. Anand could tell it was running out of oil. He reached for the bottle to refill it, then remembered that it was empty. He'd been supposed to buy some oil, too, on his way home, but the wind and the fog and the fear had driven it out of his mind.

The lamp wavered and went out. Now there were only the blue flames from the kerosene stove.

"Maybe I can help," the old man said. He rummaged in his bag and came up with the stub of a candle. It wasn't much, Anand thought as he lighted it, but at least it would last through dinner.

"I've a couple of other things here that you may be able to use," the man said. He held up a small yellow squash and a handful of green beans, and Anand thankfully chopped them up and threw them into the pot. The room began to fill with a delicious smell. As though, Anand thought, he'd put lots of expensive spices into the pot. They sat in the small golden circle of light thrown out by the candle stub, waiting for the lentils to cook. As they waited, the old man told them his story.

THE SILVER VALLEY

"My story begins long before you or I were born," the old man said, "when this city that is called Kolkata today was a swamp where tigers roamed. It begins six thousand years ago in a hidden valley of the Himalayas—the Silver Valley, as it is called by those who know it. The Silver Valley! Even now it is the most beautiful place in the world, protected by the jagged, icy swords of the mountains that form a ring around it. Only a few people know the secret passes that lead into its fragrant groves and the shining lakes of clearest water from which it takes its name. Here, many ages ago, a group of men with special powers came together with the dream of perfecting those powers and using them to further goodness in the world. They called themselves the Brotherhood of Healers, and over the centuries they taught their powers to other young men who came to them, called or chosen from among many."

"What kinds of powers?" Anand asked, fascinated. He wasn't sure he believed what the old man was saying. It sounded a bit like the fairy tales his mother used to tell him when she had the time for such things. But he was happy to listen to any story that involved magic.

"Powers of the mind," the old man said. He put out his forefinger and touched Anand lightly in the center of his forehead. "There are worlds upon worlds of power in there, far beyond what you can imagine. The Healers knew how to draw upon them."

"What can the Healers do?"

"Some can look into the future and advise men and women of what to do, and what to avoid. Some can cure sicknesses of the body and mind. Some transport themselves to places thousands of miles away. Some travel through time to bygone ages. Some know special chants to create rain or storm—or wind and fog—"

"Like the wind and fog outside?"

The old man nodded. For a second his eyes shone golden in the candle's light. "Others can make riches fall from the sky. And once in a great while, a Healer will know how to use the conch."

The old man's words vibrated through the small room. They made the hairs on Anand's arms stand up.

"The conch!" He spoke slowly, savoring the sound of the words in his mouth. "What's that?"

"It came out of an ancient time, the time of myth, when, it is said, great heroes roamed the earth. These heroes were the sons of gods—and their fathers often gave them magical gifts. Two such heroes were named Nakul and Sahadev. Their fathers, the Ashwini Kumars, who were the physicians of the gods, gave them the conch. With it, Nakul and Sahadev could heal both men and animals and cure the land of famine and drought. At the great battle of Kuru Kshetra, it is said, they even used it to bring dead warriors back to life. But in doing this, they overstepped their bounds, and in punishment the conch was taken from them and buried deep in a valley of the Himalayas, for the gods felt that men were not ready for such a gift. For centuries it lay there, lost, while armies and factions warred across the land, killing and maiming and laying the earth bare." The old man paused.

"What happened then?"

"We don't know. The early part of the story is written in the Book of Heroes, but then the trail is lost. Perhaps, when time changed and the fourth age of man—the ink-dark Kali Yug that we now live in—began, it was time for the conch to be found again. Maybe it was a hill tribe, digging for roots, that discovered it. They would not have known how to use the conch, but they recognized it as an object of power. Maybe they brought it to a holy man, a sadhu meditating near the source of the Ganges. And perhaps he glimpsed a small part of its greatness and gave it to a favorite disciple, someone with the potential to use that greatness in the service of mankind. All we know for certain is that when the Brotherhood was started six thousand years ago, the conch was already present in the center of the Silver Valley, housed inside a crystal shrine. Around it the Healers built a meditation hall where they met each dawn. Though no one except the Keeper of the Conch was permitted to handle it, each Healer knew how sacred it was, and how potent. They knew that its presence alone made it possible for them to renew their own powers each day. They also knew that these powers were not theirs to use for selfish ends."

The stranger's face grew sorrowful, and he gazed at a spot above Anand's head as though there were images drawn in the shadows that only he could see.

"But once in a while there came a Healer who grew to covet the conch's power and wanted it for himself, to bring himself glory. In the past, when the Brotherhood was stronger and more attuned to one another, such a man would be discovered immediately and reprimanded. And if he did not see the wrongness of his desire and repent, he would be sent away, with a spell laid on him so that he could never return to the valley. But in Kali Yug, the time of disintegration and darkness, the Brotherhood was diminished, for many of the masters felt they were needed down in the plains, to ease the suffering of humanity by mingling among them. And perhaps we were not as careful of whom we admitted to the Brotherhood, for interest in the healing arts—and indeed the belief in them—had waned. We were badly in need of new students to whom the knowledge could be passed along. And that was how *he* came to us."

Here the old man paused as though he were listening to something. Anand, too, listened, but he could hear nothing but the wind.

"Who are you talking about?" he asked.

"His name is Surabhanu, though it is with reluctance that I name him for you. For in spite of the yantras, the protective runes I've drawn in the corners of the room, he is sure to hear the echo of his name and sense where I am. And in my present condition, I don't have enough power left to face him again."

Anand looked curiously at the old man. There were so many questions he yearned to ask. He wanted to know more about the valley, to which he was strangely drawn. In its loveliness, it seemed to him the exact opposite of this claustrophobic tenement that he hated so much. He wanted to learn more about the Brotherhood, too. It seemed to be a new and wonderful kind of family, one that spread its protective arms around you and never went away somewhere and left you behind.

But he chose the most urgent question. "Why does Sura—this man want to find you?" As he spoke, he had a strange feeling—almost as though a slimy tentacle had touched the back of his neck. He shuddered.

The old man gave him a shrewd glance. "You felt that, didn't you? That is the finger of his attention, sweeping this area of the city. In spite of the covering I've thrown over myself, he guesses I am somewhere here, in the tenements. And when we speak of him, even without saying his name, it creates a certain connection between us. But let me finish the story quickly—I fear time is running out.

"He came to us, enchanting us with his youth and beauty, the sweetness of his nature, and the passion with which he wanted to learn. We thought that in him we had found our next Keeper of the Conch, and this was important because our current Keeper was old, and ill with a wasting disease that made him suffer much. And so we gave the young man duties and responsibilities beyond what he was ready for. Perhaps our mistake began there. We allowed him to spend as much time with the conch as he wanted so that he could study its special qualities and learn how to invoke them. At what stage the dark changes in him began, I don't know. Already he had learned enough spells to hide them from us. Or perhaps we didn't see them because we wanted so desperately to believe in him. But slowly he began speaking to one or two of the Brotherhood—those who were dazzled by his charisma or who had a streak of darkness sleeping inside them. He told them that our powers were far greater than we realized, and that we were wasting them in this sleepy little valley. He said we had been foolish to vow to use our powers only to serve others. Why, together we could take over the entire earth and rule it with our wisdom! Would that not be a good thing? For was the earth not in a sorry state, overcrowded with foolish or evil men and women who needed to be subdued and guided? Then the Golden Age might return again."

The old man sighed. "Ah, yes, he was clever enough to promise them goodness, and a return of Satya Yug, the first age, age of truth. He spoke so persuasively that most of them did not remember that goodness does not covet power or break the vows it has made.

"But one or two of the Healers he had misjudged. And they spoke to some others, and they to more, until he was called before the council, who questioned him. After much debate, it was decided that he must leave the Brotherhood the next day, and he, seeming to understand his error, agreed to do so. But he disappeared that very night, breaking through our shields—and with him he took the conch! In the morning when we came together to meditate, we found the crystal shrine cracked and empty. And worse— the old Keeper, who must have tried to stop him, was sprawled across the threshold of the hall, dead."

The old man gazed at the floor, silent, until it seemed to Anand that he had forgotten where he was.

Anand was reluctant to disturb him in his sorrow. But he, too, now had the feeling that time was running out.

"And then?" he urged.

"The council knew that without the conch, the Brotherhood would soon crumble. Already we were forgetting the chants and gestures of power, and when we

tried to send our vision over the earth, we saw only patch-
es of gray. More importantly, they knew that in the thief's
hands the conch would be gravely dangerous. If he learned
how to use it to its utmost capacity, he would unleash disaster across all the worlds, the seen and the unseen. So the
Chief Healer summoned the senior-most of the masters—
there were eight of us—and sent us, in pairs, to search the
four directions.

"My partner and I were sent south. I would need many
hours to tell you how long we traveled and how hard we
searched, and how, finally, we found the thief, disguised as
he was. Or with what difficulty we entered his domain,
eluded his followers, and stole away the conch—for with
the conch in his possession, we dared not challenge him to
a battle. Enough to say that now I have the conch with me,
and my task—an urgent one—is to return it to its proper
place."

"But where's your partner?" Anand couldn't help asking.

"Dead." The old man's voice was heavy. "He sacrificed
himself, staying back to battle the thief so that I could
escape with the conch. He was like my brother—we had
come to the Silver Valley in the same year, and had trained
together—" His eyes blazed for a moment. To Anand they
looked white, like metal that is very hot. Then the old man
lowered his head. "I can't squander my powers—reduced
as they are now—on thoughts of sorrow or revenge. I

must stay focused on my task. But to succeed, I need your help."

"*My* help!" Anand's voice was squeaky with disbelief. "How can *I* help you?"

"I need an assistant, someone to journey with me. To protect my back, as it were. There are things I'm not able to do that you might be able to do for me. Places you might be able to enter. And if there comes a time when the thief does catch up with me, you might be able to get away with the conch. Because no one would expect a mere boy to be the Conch Bearer."

Conch Bearer! The words resonated inside Anand like peals from a distant bell. More than anything else, he wanted to accept the old man's offer. But was he—the boy whom Haru yelled at every day for being slow and stupid, whom passing schoolchildren laughed at because of his torn, mismatched clothes—good enough to be a Master Healer's assistant?

"Why did you choose me?" he stammered. "I don't have any special powers. How can I help you stop the conch thief, or protect you from him?"

"I don't expect you to do that. Even I, trained as I am, couldn't do it for my brother Healer, could I? But I was called to you because of your belief in magic—and your desire to enter its secret domain."

"You heard my wish?" Anand asked incredulously. "But how—"

"At another time, I will explain all, my curious young man! For now, let me just say, yes, I heard. But more importantly, the conch seemed to hear, too. I could sense it turning its attention to you. Who knows? Maybe it sensed in you a special gift that neither you nor I know of yet. And when you touched my hand earlier today, giving me the tea, I felt your kindness. That itself is a valuable gift."

"Do you really think so?" Anand asked hesitantly. He still didn't feel valuable in any way.

The old man nodded. Then he added, "Will you come with me?"

"Yes!" Anand said, clasping his hands. His entire face shone with excitement and delight. "Oh, yes!" It seemed to him that the old man's offer was what he had been longing for all this time. This was the opportunity he'd dreamed of through these interminable months of living in the tenements. Of putting up with Haru's taunts; of seeing his mother grow sadder and sadder, wilting like a plucked flower; of being unable to help his sister as she moved further from them into the world inside her head. Not that he'd ever actually believed that it was possible to live such a life of adventure and magic. Not for him, anyway. And yet—here it was, his own, special chance to do something amazing and brave, to break through the despair and ugliness that surrounded him!

Then he remembered, and it was as though a heavy

door had slammed shut in his face. "I can't go," he said flatly. "I can't leave my mother all alone. She needs me. How would she ever take care of everything by herself?"

"Ah yes, your mother," the old man said. "Of course, you must discuss this with her when she comes home. Meanwhile, I do believe dinner is ready."

WHAT ANAND SAW

Anand ladled out heaped spoonfuls of rice and lentil stew onto tin plates and served the old man and then his sister. When he took a mouthful he was surprised at how good it was. He'd been throwing rice and lentils together almost every night for a whole year, and it had never tasted smooth and buttery like this, with a delicate hint of cumin and cardamom and cloves, the spices his mother used to use when they had had money. He was also surprised by how much of it there was—sufficient for all of them to have seconds without worrying whether there would be enough for his mother. He hadn't eaten this much in months.

When they had finished, the old man belched with satisfaction. "A lovely khichuri that was!" he said. "And now for dessert . . . ."

"I'm afraid I don't—" Anand began apologetically. But the man was busy rummaging once more in his bag.

"I think I have something in here that you may like. Ah, here it is!"

In his hand was a mango. Anand's mango!

"Where . . .? How . . .?"

The old man smiled at Anand's amazement but offered no explanation.

The mango was as sweet as Anand had imagined, and after they had each eaten a piece, and saved one for his mother, he mustered up the courage to ask something that he'd been longing to know.

"Do you have the conch with you, then?"

"I do."

"May I. . . .?" He dared not complete his request.

"See it? As a potential Conch Bearer, you certainly have that right. I'll show it to you, but what you will see will depend on who you are."

From his bag, the old man pulled out a cloth in which something was wrapped. "Just for a moment," he said. "The conch's energy is so potent that it would alert Surabhanu of its presence unless I weave a spell of disappearance around it. And I have the strength to uphold such a spell for only a very short while." He rocked back and forth, chanting, and then he opened up the cloth.

A pure light, bluish white and unlike anything Anand had ever seen, glowed out from the center of the cloth. It spread across the ground, brightening the entire room— no, transforming it, so that its walls grew into crystal and its floor silver, and its vaulted ceilings reached up beyond his sight. He heard his sister cry out behind him. But he couldn't turn to reassure her, because his eyes were held captive by what was at the center of the light.

It was a tiny conch shell, such as a child might pick up on a seashore, small enough to fit in his palm, so delicate that it seemed to be formed from the petals of jasmine flowers. And yet an enormous force throbbed from it— toward him and into him, warming him and making him lightheaded with happiness. There was music all around him, the sweetest music, as though the stars had come down from the sky and crowded into the room. He wanted to belong to this tiny, beautiful thing, to serve it forever. And yet *thing* was not the word for it, for it was more alive than most people he knew. Now he understood why the Healers were ready to die in their quest to return the conch to its rightful place. He understood, too, why the thief Surabhanu had risked everything to possess it. He put out his hand to touch it, not knowing that he did so. But the old man had pulled the cloth over the conch, covering up the beautiful light, and changing the crystal room back into the ugly shack Anand knew so well.

For a brief moment, a terrible rage came over Anand. How dare the old man take his conch away from him! He wanted to lunge forward and snatch it from his hand and hold it tightly to his chest.

"Peace, peace," the man said softly. "Not yet. You are not ready. That time will come soon enough, I'm afraid."

The red mist of rage cleared from Anand's eyes, and he

covered his face in his hands, mortified. But the man said, "Don't be ashamed. Few have looked on the beauty of the conch without desiring it. But now we have only a few more minutes before your mother returns, and I wish to speak to your sister." He beckoned to Meera. "Come and sit here, child."

Anand expected Meera to cower back, but she began to move forward slowly, with the crablike gait she had recently adopted. When she was seated in front of him, the old man reached out and gently touched her on the temples. His lips moved soundlessly. To Anand's amazement, Meera didn't flinch away but gazed at him as though she could hear what he was saying. In the flickering glow of the candle, her eyes, usually unfocused, seemed to shimmer with understanding.

What was he doing?

As though he had heard Anand's unspoken question, the old man said, "Each of the Healers of the Silver Valley is trained in many arts. But according to each one's temperament, he develops one special power. Mine is the power of remembrance and forgetting."

Anand must have looked puzzled, for the old man added, "It means that I can help people to remember what they need to remember, and forget what is better for them to forget. Your sister was stuck in a terrible moment in her past, unable to move beyond it. She had witnessed something horrifying—a man murdering another. . . ."

How had he known? Anand wondered. No one around here spoke of it.

"She'd gone to get water from the tube well near the crossroads in the late afternoon, after coming back from school," the old man continued. "Hadn't she?"

Anand nodded. "We'd just moved here. We didn't think it would be dangerous. The other children in the tenement went everywhere on their own."

"It was just bad luck," the old man said. "Your mother and you shouldn't blame yourselves. Meera had filled her pitcher and was about to cross the road when she saw a man running toward her. There was a black car coming fast behind him, as though it was chasing him. When the man was just a few feet away from your sister, the car hit him and sent him flying—"

"—and killed him," Anand whispered. "Then the car sped away. Meera saw it all happen. We found her sitting there on the pavement . . . by then the police had taken the body away."

The old man closed his eyes and wrinkled his forehead, as though he was seeing the scene against his closed lids. "Her dress was stained with the dead man's blood."

Anand nodded. "She hasn't talked to us since then."

"Those who know of such things whisper that the car belonged to a local gangster," the old man said, "a man who was so powerful that the death was never investigated."

"And, of course, no officials cared about what happened

to my sister, or did anything to help us. Oh, if only you'd known Meera the way she was before! She was so much fun, always cheering us up when we were sad."

"I can see it," the old man said. "She is still there, beneath the sadness that is covering her like an iron blanket, not letting her through." His hands moved slowly over Meera's head, as though they were feeling for something.

"It was a horrifying shock," he continued. "To see a man die in agony, and to know that the death was a result of another man's cold hatred. That this is what people are capable of doing! No child should have to face such a harsh reality!" He made a lifting motion with his hands, then added, "I'm taking the memory away from her. She will become, once more, her old lighthearted self. But patience! It takes a little time for the process to work." He turned to Meera and stroked her hair. "Be happy, child," he said.

Just then the tin door rattled.

"It's mother!" Anand said. He ran to the door and opened it eagerly.

"Am I glad to get home!" his mother said, shivering as she wrung water from her wet sari. "I got caught in the worst thunderstorm. A thunderstorm at this time of the year! I've never seen such a thing in all my days! My, it's certainly nice and warm in here."

"Maa!" Anand cried. "You'll never believe what has happened—and who's here."

"Is it your . . . father?" Anand's mother asked, a look of desperate hope on her thin face.

Anand shook his head guiltily. *I should be more careful about the words I choose!* he thought. But he'd been so excited to share the amazing events of the last few hours with his mother, that he'd just let the sentence tumble from his mouth.

His mother was peering into the room, a suspicious frown on her face.

"Who's he?" she asked. "And what's he doing?"

The old man was still smoothing down Meera's hair. Anand's mother rushed in and pulled Meera away from him. It wasn't easy. Meera struggled against her mother, making an angry guttural sound in her throat.

"He's done something bad to her," Anand's mother cried. "I know it! That's why she's making this terrible noise. Oh, my God, what shall I do now?"

"No, no, Maa," Anand said, trying to pull her back. "Don't be scared. He's a good man, a Healer. He's trying to cure Meera. He came all the way from the Silver Valley, up in the Himalayas, and battled the traitor and recovered the magic conch. . . ." His voice faltered. He could see the disbelief on his mother's face. He couldn't blame her for it. But he made himself go on. "He's come here to ask me to help him return the magic conch to the Brotherhood. I want to go with him, Mother, I really want to! Will you give me permission?"

"What are you talking about?" his mother said. "Have you gone mad?" She turned to the man. "I don't know who you are, or what nonsense you've filled my son's head with. Just because he's a child, you think you can trick him with your tales!"

"But Mother, he helped Meera. He says she's going to be cured!"

His mother put her hand on Meera's chin and turned her face to the light. "Meera, baby," she called. "Meera?"

But Meera made no response. Her lips were slack and her eyes as vacant as before.

"Look at her!" Anand's mother cried, her voice sharp with dismay. "He hasn't cured her! He just told you lies— lies to lure you away with him. He's probably a kidnap- per—or worse." She turned fiercely to the old man. "I want you out of my home, and I want you to stay away from my children, do you hear? If I see you again, I'll call the neigh- bors and make sure you get a beating you won't forget."

Anand looked in dismay from his mother to the old man, waiting for him to say something in his defense. But he merely gathered his bag and stood up.

"I don't blame you for not believing me," he said to her. "You've been through many difficulties and lost faith in the person you trusted the most. Everything I said to Anand is true. But I have no way of proving it."

"Show her the conch!" Anand said. "Then she'll have to believe you!"

The old man shook his head. "The conch is not for everyone to see."

"Please!" Anand said. "She's not 'everyone,' she's my mother! And I can't go with you unless she agrees."

"Very well," the old man said. "I do this against my will, because you ask, even though I fear it will do no good."

He took out the cloth and opened it again as he chanted. Once more a brilliant light spread across the room, though now it pulsed with a reddish glow as though the conch was displeased. Anand craned his neck to see the conch. Was it as beautiful as he remembered? But the light was so bright that it hurt his eyes, forcing him to throw his arm over them, and he saw nothing.

"What's this, old man?" he heard his mother cry. "What are you doing with that dirty piece of bone wrapped in a rag? Is it one of your voodoo objects? Is that how you hypnotized my son? Well, it won't work on me! Now, out of here before I shout for the neighbors!"

"I must go now," the old man said to Anand. "I will wait for you at Panchu's Rooming House just north of the Shyam Tala post office—but I can't wait long. At sunrise tomorrow, I'll have to start on my journey—with or without you."

He drew his thin white shawl around him and opened the door, As he stepped out into the rain, a gust of wind rushed into the room and extinguished the candle. By the time Anand's mother found it and lit it again, he was gone.

◈

Anand lay in bed in the dark, thinking over the day's events. After the old man had left, he had served his mother dinner and waited expectantly as she ate. But she hadn't said anything.

Finally, he couldn't stay silent anymore. "Do you like the khichuri, Maa?" he asked.

She had looked up from the food, a look of mild surprise on her tired face.

"Yes, son, of course I do, like always. You've really learned to cook it well. I guess you've had lots of practice these last few months! I wish we could afford something better. But you're such a good, helpful boy to me, to have dinner done by the time I get back—"

"But mother," Anand interrupted. "Doesn't it taste . . . different today?"

His mother took another mouthful and chewed thoughtfully. "Not that I can tell," she said. "Why do you ask?"

Anand didn't say anything. But a cold lump of disappointment filled his chest. Disappointment and fear. Had he then imagined everything earlier, when the old man was here? Had the old man hypnotized him, just as his mother accused him of doing? Was even the beautiful conch nothing but a figment of his fantasy?

"You've got to be more careful who you let into the house, son," his mother was cautioning him. "There are so many bad men around, tricksters and worse. You can't believe anything they tell you. Why, just the other day the laundry woman was saying that the police had caught a gang that kidnapped children and sold them in far-off places." She shuddered and her eyes filled with tears. "It really scared me, thinking of all those children, stolen from their parents, forced to live under who-knows-what conditions. If something like that happened to the two of you, I think I'd go mad. You're all I have left." Her voice broke a little, and she put an arm around each of them.

His mother was right, Anand thought as he pulled the patched bedsheet up to his neck. You can't believe what people say. The old man was a trickster, a fast talker, a cheap two-bit magician waving his arms and hypnotizing children, luring them with impossible stories and false hopes. Who knows what he had planned to do to Anand once he got him away from home? It was a good thing Anand's mother had arrived when she did. She'd seen right through him and sent him packing—and he hadn't even had anything to say in his defense. The worst part— even worse than tricking him with the . . . but what was it that the old man had shown him? Somehow Anand just couldn't remember. The worst part was promising them that Meera would be better. Because she wasn't. When mother had tucked her into her pallet, wishing her good night, she had stared vaguely at the ceiling as she always did, without responding.

Anand wiped his eyes and tried to go to sleep, but the tears kept coming. He wasn't sure why he was crying. Was it for Meera, trapped forever inside her head, or for his mother, who worked so hard and achieved so little, or for his own broken hopes of escaping from the dull grind of his everyday life into a world of adventure and mystery?

He wept silently, taking care that his mother did not hear. He was glad that the rain beating down on their corrugated tin roof, and the angry peals of thunder, which sounded as though they were very close, were loud enough to drown out any muffled sobs that might escape him. Finally, exhausted, he fell into an uneasy sleep.

THE MESSAGE

Anand stood on a mountain peak, wrapped in a robe the color of blood. Was it *his* blood the robe was colored with? There was an animal with him—he wasn't sure what kind it was. He could glimpse only a bushy golden tail out of the corner of his eye. A storm was approaching the mountain—no, it was *him* the storm was approaching, *him* it was aimed at. He watched it roll across the sky, sounding like the iron wheels of a hundred gigantic chariots, staining the land beneath it with grayness. He could see dark clouds torn by lightning, could see hailstones dropping from them like crystal bullets. He knew it was no ordinary storm. There was something darker at the center of it, a malevolence—and it wanted him. Or perhaps it was what he held in his hands that it wanted. The force of its wanting filled the air with a rotten stench. He looked around desperately for someone—*who?* Whoever it was, he wasn't there. *What shall I do?* he cried out. But only the wind answered. It sounded like the siren of an ambulance, hinting at disaster. He raised up his arms and spoke the words that rose to his mouth, though he didn't know what they meant. Whatever was in his hands burst into flame, though it was not a flame that scorched him. No, the flame was bitter cold. It traveled down his arms and into his chest like an old ache, and when it reached his heart, a whirlwind of ice rose around him. He knew then that he had done the wrong thing, the wrongest, most dangerous thing he could do, by calling upon the power of that which he held in his hand, which had never been meant for his use. The whirlwind of ice sucked at the edges of the storm, pulling the darkness into itself. Anand watched, horrified, unable to stop it. Once the black center of the storm merged with the white center of the whirlwind, he knew, the world would explode into nothingness. Already the storm's claws were digging into his upper arm, shaking him, not letting go no matter how much he screamed and thrashed about—

"Brother! Brother!"

Anand opened his eyes. He was lying on his pallet in his one-room shack, and Meera was leaning over him, shaking him by the arm. "Brother!" she said urgently as he stared at her, confused, still entangled in the dream, his heart still beating too fast. "Wake up! It's morning! You're late already."

Was his sister really speaking, or had he merely exchanged one dream for another, happier one? No, here was the cold concrete floor, and the puddle of water that always formed near the window after a heavy rain.

"Meera?" he whispered, afraid to trust his ears. "Are you—?"

She nodded, the excited grin he remembered so well lighting up her face. "I'm me again!" She spun around, too happy to stand still. "When I woke up this morning, it was like someone had pulled away a big, black blanket that had been wrapped tight around me all this time."

Anand jumped up from his pallet. Beyond Meera's head he could see his mother's face, alight with incredulous joy.

"Our Meera!" he said to her. "She's cured!"

His mother nodded, smiling, wiping at her eyes. "Yes, thanks be to God! At first I didn't dare to believe it, but it's true. She has been chattering away ever since she woke me up."

"Then the old man—?"

She looked away, but not before he saw the reluctance in her eyes. She was silent for a long time. He could see, in the stiffness of her shoulder blades, that she didn't want to answer his question. He knew she was afraid that if she did so, she would lose him. But she was an honest woman, so after a moment she took a deep breath and turned to Anand. "He spoke the truth. He was a Healer."

"Then the rest of his story must be true as well," Anand cried in agitation. "I must go to him! I must help him!" He hesitated, his heart torn between two kinds of yearning the way it had never been before. "But how can I leave you alone?"

For a moment his mother said nothing. Then, reluctantly, she whispered, "Go! I will be fine. We owe it to the Healer—and I can see that you long to join him."

Anand's heart leaped with joy, and he couldn't stop a smile from breaking over his face. Hurriedly, he washed his face and pulled on a clean shirt. Meera brought over his sandals and shawl, and a bit of leftover khichuri that she had wrapped in leaves, and gave him a hug.

"Don't fret," she said. "I'll be here with Maa . . . I'll help her."

"I know you will," he replied, smiling at the familiar, determined look in her eyes. How wonderful it was to have his sister back! How much he'd missed her all these months! He wished he could stay longer, but already, from the bit of light that straggled in through the wire mesh of the shack's lone window, he could tell it was long past sunrise. There were so many things he wanted to say to his mother and sister before leaving— how much he loved them, how he would worry about them no matter what they said. How he would miss them even in the midst of the greatest adventure of his life. But there was no time. Perhaps it was already too late.

He hugged his sister and touched his mother's feet for blessing.

"Don't worry about me," he said. "The old man will take good care of me, I'm sure. I'll come back as soon as I can. And when I do, why, I'm sure he'll give me all kinds of rich and wonderful gifts to bring back to you."

Meera clapped her hands. "Will you bring me back a princess doll, Brother, dressed in a red silk sari?"

"I will," Anand promised. He glanced at his mother, but she did not say anything. She only laid her hand on his head in the traditional gesture of blessing. He could see she was trying not to cry. That was when he came closest to not leaving. Perhaps she saw it in his eyes, for she took him by the shoulders and led him to the door and gave him a little push.

"Godspeed," she said.

Only later, when he was halfway to Shyam Tala post office, did Anand realize she hadn't said what she always said to him when he went somewhere. *Come back safely, and soon.* As though she had no hope of his return.

Standing in front of the post office, Anand looked around confusedly, his breath coming in gasps. He had run all the way, but now that he was here, where was Panchu's Rooming House? It struck him that though he often passed by the post office, he'd never noticed a rooming house. He walked back and forth several times past the post office, peering closely at the shops and alleyways that surrounded it. There was only Ramlal's sweets store, the Jai Durga bike repair shop, and a soft drink stall, its shelves lined with brightly colored bottles of Jusla and Thumbs Up. He wished he'd asked the old man for directions. But he'd been too busy doubting him.

Finally, he plucked up enough courage to ask the soft-drink man if he knew where the rooming house was. But the man frowned and shook his head. "Never heard of it," he said.

Anand closed his eyes, a sick feeling of despair washing over him. *I'm sorry*, he cried inside his head. *Help me find you.* He tried to conjure up the old man's face in his mind, but nothing would come. Nothing except a flash of bluish light. Where had he seen something like that before? He couldn't remember. He opened his eyes to find that a couple of the shopkeepers were eyeing him suspiciously.

Just then a girl of about ten emerged from a gap between two of the stalls, wearing a torn wool wrapper and sweeping the street vigorously though not very effectively with a worn coconut-frond broom. Anand hadn't noticed the gap before. Now he looked closer. Why, it was a narrow passage that led to . . . what was that? It was dark inside the passageway, but Anand could have sworn he saw a cave in there, its black mouth further obscured by mist. The path to it was narrow and rocky, fringed with thorny cacti. He blinked and rubbed his eyes. All that running on an empty stomach must have made him dizzy, because now that he looked again, he saw only a black, paint-chipped door at the end of a dirty passageway lined with garbage. Could it be? Since there was nothing else he could think of doing, he walked down the passage to the door, looking around for a signboard. There was none. Hesitantly, he knocked on the door.

The door opened so quickly that Anand almost fell in. A very fat man in a dirty kurta stood there, chewing on a neem stick that served as his toothbrush. He spat expertly, close to Anand's feet, then said, with a glare, "Never any peace to be found here! What do *you* want now?"

"Is this—is this a rooming house?"

"No, it's the Parliament building!" the man snapped. "Don't you have eyes in your head?" He pointed with the bristly end of the neem stick.

There was a small black sign on the door, though Anand could have sworn it hadn't been there a moment ago. On it was printed, in straggly red letters, PANCHU'S ROOMING HOUSE. CLEAN, COMFORTABLE AND CONFIDENTIAL. YOUR HOME AWAY FROM HOME.

"And it's full, so you'd better go elsewhere," the man said, starting to shut the door in Anand's face.

Desperately, Anand wedged his foot in the doorway. "Wait! I need to contact someone who's staying here—an old man."

Was it Anand's imagination, or did the fat man look uncomfortable? "Lots of old men stay here," he said. "What's his name?"

"I—I don't know." Even to himself, Anand thought he sounded half-witted. "He wore white, and had a long beard."

The man laughed without humor. "If I had a rupee for every bearded old man who wore white!" he said. "Sorry, kid. Anyway, a couple of guests left pretty early this morning. I think there was an old man among them."

"Did he tell you where he was going? Did he leave a message with you for someone named Anand?"

"A message?" the fat man wrinkled up his forehead. "Hmmm. My memory isn't what it used to be. Now, if you had something to give me, a little gift maybe, that might jog my brain cells."

Anand started to tell the man he didn't have any money, but then he remembered. He hadn't had a chance to give his mother his week's pay. He dug in his waistband and brought out a crumpled rupee note. The man wrinkled his face in disgust. "Is that all?" he said. But he stretched out his hand for it anyway. "Well, then—"

At that moment, a gust of cold wind blew down the alley, scattering torn papers ahead of it. Maybe it was the narrowness of the alley, but the wind seemed to make a whistling sound as it came. It was cold, too, Anand thought with a shiver. A cloud must have passed over the sun, because it was suddenly darker in the alley. The fat man's eyes widened as though he saw something, but there was nothing when Anand turned to look. The man thrust the rupee back into Anand's hand. "There was no message," he said. He kicked Anand's foot out of the way and slammed the door.

Anand didn't knock again. He had a feeling it would be no use, and, more importantly, he wanted to get out of the alley as soon as he could. He started to make his way back to the main street, his head lowered against the wind. But how had the alley grown so long and winding? It was lined with black cacti that reached out to snag him with their thorns. And the main street at its end—why, he could barely see it through the tiny opening. It was hard to walk, too. The cobblestones were wet and slippery. And though the ground was flat—he knew it was—every step felt as though he were climbing a steep hill.

Then at the head of the alley, he saw the girl again. She was singing something—not in a particularly musical voice, but cheerfully and loudly—as she swept the cobbles. It was a single line she repeated, and after a moment Anand could figure out the words, though they didn't make much sense to him.

> *O ocean flower, all walled in white,*
> *how far are you from home?*
> *O ocean flower, all walled in white,*
> *how far are you from home?*

Somehow the singsong voice gave Anand a sense of comfort. He didn't feel so alone, and his steps grew stronger. As he reached the girl, he gave her a grateful smile.

The girl didn't smile back. She kept singing the strange little song. Anand couldn't tell if her eyes were friendly or not. Her short, uncombed hair hung around her face like a mane—as though she were a small, wild lion, Anand thought.

On an impulse, he said, "I'm looking for an old man with a walking stick and a beard. He was carrying a bundle—"

The girl turned to the entrance of the alley as though she hadn't heard Anand. But then she made a beckoning motion with her hand for him to follow her.

Once on the main street, the girl threw her broom under the soft-drink stall and hurried into the post office, which was bustling with clamoring customers and the loud, metallic ringing of the change machines. Anand followed, mystified. The girl grabbed him by the arm and pulled him into one of the lines. "It's safest to talk in here, with all this noise," she whispered. "He left early this morning. He told Panchu that a boy might come looking for him, a boy named Anand."

"That's me!" Anand said, his heart beating madly. "Did he say where he was going?"

The girl nodded.

"Where? Tell me—please?" When she remained silent, Anand pulled out the rupee note again.

She wrinkled her nose in disdain. "I don't do things for money," she said. "Especially not for such a pathetically small amount!" Her eyes were dark and flecked with green—and very determined. They made him uneasy.

"What I want is for you to take me along," the girl said. "Oh, it's no use frowning like that. You don't have a choice, not if you want to catch up with the old man before he's gone for good."

"You don't understand!" Anand burst out. "This isn't a game. It's really important—and I don't have time to waste. It's dangerous, too! Too dangerous for a girl."

She looked at him coldly. "That's funny, coming from a soft house-bred boy like you! I live on the streets—I play hopscotch with danger every day! You know, I could have just gone to the old man by myself and said that you hadn't shown up. Then he would have taken me along instead of you—and happily, because I'll be a far better helper to him than you."

"He'd never take you instead of me," Anand said hotly. But he wasn't sure. After all, he *had* let the old man down by disbelieving him. And he *was* late.

The girl had heard the uncertainty in his voice. She grinned. "In fact, I think that's what I'll do right now if you don't agree."

"I won't let you!" Anand said furiously.

"How are you going to stop me?" The girl faced him, hands on her thin hips. "I could be out of here before you blinked, and then you'd never find me. I know every alleyway around here. Think of it like this—I'm the one who's taking you along. Don't look so glum! I'll probably save your life several times along the way."

Anand walked in angry silence next to the girl. He had decided that he wouldn't speak to her, not even once. And as soon as he saw the old man, he would explain, in full detail, the way she had blackmailed him into bringing her along. The old man would be even angrier than Anand was. He'd throw her out—and that would serve her right.

The girl, however, didn't even notice his silence. Having gotten her way, she was as happy as a buffalo in a pond full of mud. She was telling him all about herself (not that Anand was the least bit interested) and how she came to know where the old man would be.

"I sleep in the space under the soft-drink stall," she said. "I keep the street in front of the stalls swept and clean—that's why the soft-drink man lets me stay there. He sends me on errands, too, and usually by nighttime I'm so tired I sleep like a log. Don't even dream. But last night, what with all the thunder and lightning, I kept waking up. Also, I kept getting these dreams. . . ." She shivered suddenly, as though they had been unpleasant ones, but she didn't explain further.

"So I was awake when the old man came out of the alleyway very early this morning, with Panchu following him, scraping and bowing like the man was somebody really important. It was still dark, but I could see his face clearly. It shone as though there was a light inside it, and his beard—why, it looked like it was made of silver. He told Panchu to send you straight to the Sialdah train station if you showed up in the morning—that's where he'd be, on the platform from which the Pathankot Express leaves. Then he said, 'Tell him to look where he usually wouldn't, to look with sharp eyes. It will be hard to see me. Tell him, things aren't what they seem.' Then he bent to tighten his sandal strap—he was in front of the soft-drink stall then— and he looked right into my eyes. I was scared that he'd be mad because I heard him, but he wasn't. His eyes twinkled like . . . my grandfather's used to." Here the girl stopped and cleared her throat.

Anand felt his anger recede as he wondered where her grandfather was now, and her father and mother. Living in Kolkata, he had seen street children all his life, but he'd never really thought about how they lived. Now he felt a pang as he pictured the sweeper girl curled up on rags night after night under the soft-drink stall, even when it was cold or stormy.

But the girl was speaking again. "So I thought, he must *want* me to hear it, for some reason! That's why I hung around this morning, sweeping and resweeping the street, because I didn't trust Panchu. Especially after the other one came."

"The other one?" asked Anand with a sinking feeling in his stomach.

The girl nodded, her face serious. "I didn't see him— and I didn't want to. Right after the old man left, the street-lights flickered and went out, and there was this *cold* dark-ness that moved along the street. It scared me—and I'm not easily scared, I tell you. I've seen some strange folks come to Panchu's rooming house. But this time I pushed myself as far back under the stall as I could and covered my head with my wrapper and didn't even breathe until I was sure he had passed into the alley. What happened after that, I'm not sure."

"He probably scared Panchu into telling him where the old man went," Anand said softly to himself. "And he probably ordered him not to tell me anything. That's why Panchu was afraid to take my money, even though I could see that he wanted to. And that cold wind in the alley, maybe he —or one of his followers—was keeping an eye on Panchu." A horrifying thought struck him. "Maybe he's keeping an eye on us now! Or maybe"—and he knew this would be even worse—"he's gone to the station and found the old man!"

"That's why we'd better get to the station as soon as we can," the girl said, lengthening her steps.

Something bothered Anand as he ran to catch up with her. "The evil man, the one whose presence you felt—he's really powerful. He could have stopped us—maybe even killed us—already. Why hasn't he?"

The girl shrugged. "I don't know."

As they hurried along, Anand glanced at her tough, resolute face. She was clever and resourceful, he could tell that already, and not easily scared. But could he trust her? Finally, he asked, "Why do you want to come with me? I don't even know where I'm going, or what I'll have to face. It isn't exactly a fun trip, you know, not like going on holiday—"

"It's got to be better than living under the soft-drink stall," she said. "Rats come around there sometimes at night. Man, they're as big as your head! It's a good thing I'm handy with my broomstick. Besides . . ." But then she stopped.

"What?" Anand asked.

She looked a bit embarrassed but said it anyway. "I want to see the old man again. To see if he really looks like my grandfather, or if I'd just imagined it."

"That song you were singing today—what was it?"

The girl looked blank. "Was I? I can't remember. Sometimes I hum things as I work. Makes the day go faster."

"This was just one line that you kept repeating. Something about colors and walls and flowers." Anand wrinkled his forehead, trying to remember, but the words wouldn't come to him.

The girl shrugged. "Don't know."

"What's your name, by the way?" Anand asked. But the girl was pointing ahead. "We're at the station," she said. "Let's find him."

THINGS AREN'T WHAT THEY SEEM

The huge redbrick building that made up the Sialdah Station was noisy and confusing, with hundreds of people rushing in every direction and loudspeakers blaring information about trains bound for cities all over India, cities Anand hadn't even known existed. Anand had never been here before, and he stared at the scene in front of him in amazement and dismay. In addition to the passengers, there were vendors selling watermelons and movie magazines, coolies carrying huge pieces of rolled-up bedding on their heads, and whole families of beggars who had set themselves up in strategic locations where people would trip over them—and thus be embarrassed into giving them money. How on earth in the middle of all this would he find the right platform—and the old man?

The girl pulled at Anand's arm. "Do you have money to buy tickets?"

"How much?" Anand asked anxiously.

"Probably a hundred rupees, at least." She sighed at the look on Anand's face. "Never mind, I didn't think you would. Well, it's going to be tricky getting past the ticket checker. See that mean-looking man in the black uniform at the wrought-iron gate? That's him. We'll have to wait until a big family with a lot of baggage gets there, and then try to slip in with them."

They waited. Anand's throat was dry with fear. He didn't like breaking rules—not even little ones. Besides, the ticket checker was a burly man with a thick handlebar moustache, and he didn't look like he'd have much sympathy for anyone who tried to sneak past him.

"Psst!" the sweeper girl said. "Now!"

A jovial group of ten or eleven was approaching the gate. They were well dressed and looked as though they were on their way to a special event—a wedding, maybe. The men wore gold buttons on their silk kurtas, and the women were dressed in fancy embroidered saris and had flowers in their hair. Three or four coolies followed them, carrying fat suitcases. The girl darted between the coolies and made it past the checker while he was examining the group's tickets. Anand tried to follow. He was almost past the gate when he felt a heavy arm descend on his shoulder.

"Where do you think you're going, you young ragamuffin?" a voice thundered. "And where's your ticket?"

Anand looked up into the checker's angry face. Out of the corner of his eye, he could see the girl peering worriedly from behind a pillar on one of the platforms.

"Please let me go!" he begged the checker, but the man shook his head.

"I've seen you before!" he shouted. "You're with that gang of pickpockets, aren't you? You boys are always slipping past me and getting onto trains and stealing from the passengers. Well, not today! Today I'm going to hand you over to the station police."

"I'm not part of any gang," Anand cried. "I've never even been in this station before!"

"That's what they all claim!" the checker said as he took out a huge silver whistle from his pocket. "A couple of nights in the lockup and you'll be singing a different tune."

Anand looked around desperately. Any moment now the checker was going to blow his whistle, and the police would come. Before he knew it, he'd be locked up, and probably given a solid beating as well. He'd ruined it all—he'd failed the old man and his mission even before he started.

"Excuse me, sir," someone said in a quavery voice just then. "I see my nephew got here before me. Thank you for holding on to him. I would have had the hardest time finding him if he'd gotten past the gate! Ah, here are our tickets."

It was an old man, but not the man who'd followed Anand home. Or was it? This man's beard was more gray than white, his face was narrower, and his ears were small and flat and sat close to his head. He wore a spotless white jacket with crisply ironed white pants. His lace-up shoes were so shiny with black polish that Anand could see his reflection in them.

"Your nephew, is he?" the checker said, frowning suspiciously at Anand's ragged clothes as he took the tickets and examined them.

"Yes, indeed, my very own sister's son," the old man said. "Don't you see the resemblance?" He made a small gesture with his hand and the checker's face cleared.

"Indeed, I do, now that you mention it," he said in a friendlier voice.

The old man nodded to Anand, "Come on, Nephew! Don't be fool enough to get separated from me again."

Anand stared, not sure what to do. Should he follow this stranger? He *had* gotten Anand out of a predicament. Was he the old man in disguise? He remembered the message the girl had given him: *Things are not what they seem.* But that could mean so many things.

"The Pathankot Express leaves from platform fourteen in twenty minutes, sir," the checker said, sounding positively polite now. "You'd better hurry. I see you have first-class tickets. That compartment will be toward the front of the train. Have a good journey!"

The man bowed briefly and started off, not checking to see if Anand followed. For an old man, he walked very fast, his jacket billowing in the wind. There was no time to think—already he was disappearing into the crowd. Anand ran after him. It was hard keeping up with him on the congested platform. He tried to locate the sweeper girl as he hurried along, but she was nowhere to be found. He felt a twinge of disappointment that she would not be coming with them after all.

"Ah, here we are," the man said finally. "At the far end of platform fourteen. And here's our compartment." He jumped onto the train—it was marvelous how light he was on his feet—and took a window seat. He motioned to Anand to sit across from him. "A good thing it's empty, no?" he said with a warm smile. "We have so much to talk about. But first, you must be starving! I have a feeling you left home without eating breakfast, didn't you?"

Anand nodded. How kind the old man's smile was. He was ashamed at having doubted him. Had anyone ever smiled at Anand with such understanding? There had been a woman, once—was it his mother? He couldn't quite recall. It was clear to him, though, that even she couldn't have cared for him as much as this man in front of him, who was unwrapping a large cloth filled with—Anand blinked in amazed delight—all the dishes Anand loved. There were piles of deep-fried pooris, golden brown and still steaming. There were the crisp triangles of samosas stuffed with spicy peas and potatoes, and green coriander-leaf chutney to dip them in. There was chicken cooked in yogurt sauce, and the biggest fried prawns Anand had ever seen. Next to them sat sweets of several kinds—juicy red gulab jamuns and the orange twists of jilebis, and, in a large, shining silver bowl, his absolute favorite: rice pudding studded with raisins and pistachios, which he hadn't eaten in ages and ages. His mouth watered.

"How did you know I like all these foods?" he asked as he reached for the pudding bowl and the spoon that lay next to it.

"Because they happen to be my favorite foods, too," the man said, his smile broadening. "You and I have many similarities, Anand. But more of that later! Eat now. You must be famished."

Just then Anand's eyes caught a movement outside the window. It was the sweeper girl, waving from behind a pillar. Ah! She wasn't lost after all! That was good. Anand started to call out to her to come and join them. The old man was so generous, surely he wouldn't mind. Then he realized that the girl wasn't waving. She was beckoning furiously to Anand. From time to time she pointed at her mouth and shook her head, as though telling him not to eat.

Now why would she do that? Anand wondered as he raised the spoon filled with rice pudding to his mouth. And why was she hiding behind that silly pillar, like a spy in a bad Hindi movie?

"Ah, I see that your friend has found us," the old man said, without glancing out of the window. "Good, good. Why don't you invite her to join us here?"

Anand reluctantly put down the spoon and leaned out of the window to call to her. But she was already walking toward their compartment. No, not exactly walking. It was more as though there was an invisible rope tied around her waist, and it was dragging her forward while she tried to resist. She bumped into a couple of people as she stumbled toward the compartment door, and even tried to grab hold of one of them. But the man just kept walking, as though he could neither see nor feel the girl grasping at his arm. As though the girl existed in a different world.

Anand turned to ask the old man what was going on, but what he saw made him gasp. The expression on the old man's face had changed, so that instead of a smile, there was now a sneer on it. But what was really different were his eyes. They were gray, like stones, and like stones they were opaque, so that looking into them Anand couldn't see his own reflection. There was no light in them, only a muddy darkness that waited to capture and devour anything that ventured near it.

How could he have ever mistaken this creature to be the Healer from the Silver Valley?

There was a noise at the compartment door, and then the girl stumbled in. There was a terrified look on her face, and she kept her eyes lowered, as though she knew something awful would happen if the man looked into them.

"Come here, girl," the man said. His voice was young and hard, and Anand saw that he had changed further. His face was clean-shaven and unwrinkled now, except for the deep lines that ran from his nose to the sides of his mouth. His head was clean-shaven, too, and on his forehead he wore a diadem with a red stone. His robe was a matching red as well, and fell to his feet, shimmering like flames. The fabric had a strange design on it: figures, both human and animal, caught in positions of agony. When Anand glanced at them from the corner of his eye, it looked to him as though they were writhing.

"No!" cried the girl, and she tried to hold on to the door frame. But whatever force held her jerked her toward the man. She tried to recite something in a small, stammering voice, but kept failing. At first Anand couldn't make out the words, but then he heard them.

White wall, white wall, white wall . . .

"I see that Abhaydatta tried to teach you a rhyme of protection!" the man said. "But he didn't do too good a job of it, did he? Not that it could have saved you from my power, the power of Surabhanu!" He raised a hand, and the girl dropped to the floor like a chopped-off branch.

"Help!" Anand shouted, pressing his face against the window bars and banging on them with his fists. He wasn't sure whom he was calling to, who might be able to help him. Not the passersby—they seemed oblivious to what was going on inside the compartment. And the old man—only God knew where he was when Anand needed him so desperately!

"You might as well save your strength," the man with the red diadem said with a cold laugh. "As you've probably guessed, they can't see or hear you." He raised his hand again, and it seemed to Anand as though a huge fist slammed into his throat, cutting off his voice. The pain brought him, moaning, to his knees next to the girl.

"So, you are Abhaydatta's new assistants, eh?" the man said, laughing again. "Pitiful that he's been reduced to gathering such riffraff around him! Did he really think that street urchins such as you could help him protect the treasure he's stolen from me, Surabhanu? Why, it'll be child's play to search your minds and find out if there's anything of importance that he has told you. Then I'll embed my own commands in there, so that you'll no longer be Abhaydatta's assistants, but mine! Only, he won't know that when he finds you—not until it's too late! For you'll look and act exactly as you were before." His soft, evil laugh sent a shiver along Anand's body.

Surabhanu moved a finger, and against his will Anand found himself staring into his eyes. As before, when he'd been in his shack with the old man, he felt something like a tentacle moving over him. Only this time it was slimier and much larger. It paused over his face. Anand knew that any moment it would descend, and he would feel it sucking at him. And then whatever was in him—whatever *was* him, Anand—would be taken away. And something else would be put in its place. Anand shuddered to think what that might be.

Help! he cried silently once again, trying to focus his mind on the old man's face, hoping that perhaps this way he could somehow convey his desperation—and his location—to the Healer. But instead, surprisingly, the image that filled his mind was that of the conch with its star-blue light.

The tentacle moved caressingly along his face and cheekbones. Was the same thing happening to the girl? Anand wasn't able to turn his head to look. The tentacle had paused on his lips. Its fat, moist feel made him want to scream or throw up in disgust. But he was powerless to do either. Now it attached itself to his temple, and he felt it beginning to suck. At the same time, something burning hot was entering his head through the same place, which began to throb. He closed his eyes hopelessly.

Then, from somewhere far away, he heard a voice. It sounded like it belonged to a teenaged boy.

"Sweet colored lozenges!" it called. "Sugar-dipped lozenges! Lemon-orange-mango, lemon-orange-mango! The best you've ever tasted!"

The voice was getting closer. Now it seemed to be in the passageway outside their compartment.

The tentacle paused. The suction lessened, then stopped. Surabhanu glared at the doorway.

"What's this?" he muttered. "No one but a master

magician can penetrate the sheath I've placed around this space. Could it be Abhaydatta?" His brow creased as he sniffed the air. "The energy coming from this one is different. But it could be a trick. It would be just like the old fool to come bursting in here, playing the hero to rescue these two miserable creatures, when he could be halfway to the Silver Valley with the—" Here his mouth twisted in rage and he left the sentence unfinished.

"Well, if it is him," he said after a moment with his sneering smile, "all the better. I'll catch three birds in one throw of the net."

"Lemon-pineapple," the voice said, "banana-coconut. Twenty for a rupee, a deal you can't beat! For old, for young! My lozenges will change your life!"

A tall, gangly boy came into the room, dressed in the knee-length dhoti and shirt that most vendors wore. Hanging from his neck was a tray filled with powdered sugar on which lay candies of many colors. He gave the three of them—the man in his red cloak and the two children at his feet—a buck-toothed grin as though there was nothing unusual in what he saw. "Lozenges for all! Special lozenges for all!"

Could it be the old man? Even twenty-four hours back, Anand would have scoffed if anyone had suggested such a thing to him, but now he wasn't sure. A curtain had parted, letting him into a world where he could no longer depend on his eyes to tell him the truth. He stared at the boy, trying to see if he recognized something about him—maybe a gesture or a particular way of turning his head—but there was nothing, Then he realized something else. He had just turned his head! And the girl was cautiously flexing her arms. When Surabhanu's attention had transferred itself from them to the newcomer, his spell had weakened enough to allow them to move.

Surabhanu straightened to his full height until his head seemed to touch the compartment's ceiling. "Abhaydatta!" he cried in a terrible voice. "Fool! Now you'll feel the full force of my powers!"

"What are you talking about, babuji?" the boy asked, looking scared and backing toward the door. "If you don't want my sweets, that's okay. I can go—"

"Not so fast!" Surabhanu said. "I don't know how you got in here, whoever you are. But you'll soon find out that you can't leave until I will it." He made a fist with his left hand and raised it high. Anand watched in horrified sympathy as the boy stumbled and fell forward. The lozenges flew up from his tray, and powdered sugar filled the air like a fine white mist.

But what was this? Instead of falling to the ground, the candies flew through the air like shards of brightly colored glass, straight at Surabhanu. He batted at them wildly, but they stuck to his face. Some covered his eyes and some entered his mouth, causing him to gag. Anand stared, openmouthed, as Surabhanu tried to pluck them off his skin, yelling with pain. He looked around for the candy seller, but the haze of powdered sugar had filled the compartment, obscuring most of it.

He felt a hand in his, tugging. It was the sweeper girl.

"Come on," she whispered.

He struggled to his feet. The haze had covered Surabhanu now so that he was only a faint, thrashing silhouette. Was there another figure in there, tangled up with him? Anand didn't have the time to check. The two of them ran as fast as they could through the door, off the train, and down the platform. They ran all the way across the station and outside, not caring which way they went, bumping into travelers who shouted curses at them. Finally, they collapsed in a breathless heap on the pavement outside. Anand looked over his shoulder fearfully, half expecting to see an enraged Surabhanu at his heels, arms outstretched to grab him. But there was no one. For the moment, they had escaped!

Anand wanted to dance for joy—but then his heart sank. If the candy seller was really their old man, maybe he was in deep trouble. Should they have stayed back and tried to help him instead of running away? But now they didn't dare go back into the station to look for him. And sooner or later Surabhanu would break free of the sugar-candy spell and come after them. What were they to do?

THE MEETING POINT

Anand looked around helplessly, hoping for a sign. I need something to guide me to the right choice, he thought. So far, I've just made one mistake after another. Station life flowed around him as usual. Passengers, porters, bus drivers, vendors, and policemen hurried by, intent on their business, oblivious to the two children who sat on the dirty concrete near the station gates. But Anand thought it would probably be a good idea to move away from the entrance.

The girl pointed at a corner wall where a food vendor had set up his stand and was doing brisk business. "I'm starving, aren't you? I think we can get a couple of packets of puffed rice for a rupee."

Anand tried to remember exactly how many rupees he had with him—he didn't want to take them out in plain sight of everyone. The pickpockets the guard had spoken of were probably lurking around a corner.

The girl seemed to know what he was thinking. "Don't worry," she said, with a shrewd glance, as though she knew his thoughts. "You'll still have enough money left for a few more meals. By then, we'll either find our old man, or we'll go back home—or that weird guy will catch us, and that'll put an end to all our worries!"

Anand couldn't help giving a shudder at her words. But she only laughed and began to push her way through the crowd. He didn't know quite what to make of her. How could anyone shrug off such a frightening experience so casually? He stood silently, watching and wondering, while she bargained firmly for two packets of spicy puffed rice, making the vendor add a handful of chopped onions at no extra cost.

The puffed rice was delicious and tangy with chilies and lemon juice. Anand took several large, appreciative mouthfuls of it. He hadn't realized until now just how hungry he was. The girl was off again—this time to find a tea seller. "Hurry," she called over her shoulder. "You can't really enjoy puffed rice unless you have a hot cup of tea to wash it down with. Come on, cheapskate! It'll cost only a few paise."

Trying to keep up with her as he took another large mouthful of the rice, Anand didn't see where he was stepping. The next thing he knew, he was down on the floor, sprawled across a large, ragged bundle.

"Ow! Ow! Ow!" cried the bundle. "Killed a poor blind woman, he has, the ruffian!"

Anand jumped up and stared. He had tripped over an

old beggar woman—at least he thought it was a woman there, under the filthy, tattered shawl that covered a thin body and part of a face. Greasy, stringy hair fell into the woman's eyes. Anand drew in a startled breath—the pupils of the eyes were milky white instead of black. The woman was, indeed, blind. He felt horribly guilty.

The woman wrung her bony hands and moaned. "He's broken my leg, as surely as God is in heaven! How will I manage to get back and forth now? I'll starve in my hovel, unable to even go begging!"

Anand knelt down, overcome with remorse. "Where does it hurt?" he asked. "Let me take a look at your leg—"

"No! No!" the woman whined. "You'll only make it worse. If you really want to help, just give me some money and be on your way."

Anand was about to put a rupee note in the battered tin bowl the woman held out to him, when the girl's voice broke in, startling him. She must have come back to see why Anand had fallen behind.

"Don't give her a single paisa!" she shouted. "I know these station beggars. It's all a trick—she probably does the same thing twenty times a day."

She, too, knelt down and put her face close to the woman's. "You cheat!" she hissed. "Tripping innocent passers by with your staff, then pretending they've hurt you so they'll give you money! Why I bet you're not even blind."

Anand stared at her, startled by her vehemence. The woman was old, after all, and must be very poor as well. Why else would anyone put up with the curses and insults that were regularly heaped on beggars? He would have expected the girl to be more sympathetic to another homeless person. It struck him with a sense of misgiving that he didn't really know her at all.

The girl raised her hand in a sudden movement, and the woman flinched back and hid her face behind her arm.

"Just as I thought," the girl said triumphantly. "She can see quite well."

"Well enough to see that you have a black heart," the woman muttered. To Anand, she added, "Don't trust her, young man! I'd advise you to get away from her as soon as you can."

"When we want your advice, we'll ask you for it!" the girl said. She grabbed Anand's arm. "Come on, let's get our tea."

But Anand couldn't just turn his back on the beggar woman. Even if she wasn't really blind, it must still be hard for her to spend the last years of her life on a station platform. Did she not have any children who could take care of her? For a moment he pictured his own mother in a similar situation and fear twisted inside him sharply, like the blade of a knife. He bent and placed a rupee note in the woman's bowl.

"That was dumb!" the girl cried. "*We* needed that money!"

Anand didn't reply, but he felt good about what he'd done.

"Thank you for your kindness, young man," the woman wheezed. "In return, I'll tell you something to help you. That which is lost may often be found at the meeting point." She gathered her bowl and staff and rose creakingly to her feet.

"What's the meeting point?" Anand asked.

"Never heard of it," the girl said. "Ignore her. They like to talk nonsense, these beggars, just to get your attention."

"Ah," said the old woman to the girl. "Maybe you haven't heard of everything there is to hear." To Anand she said, "It's at the great banyan tree that stands in the center of the Esplanade, where the buses leave from. Those who know that things are not what they seem are familiar with it." And with that she hobbled off, weaving her way dexterously through the crowd.

"If that woman's blind, then I'm the Queen of England," the girl exclaimed, but Anand was already walking to the bus stop.

"I don't know if we should trust—" she started to say.

"That message was meant to come to us," he said, his voice confident.

"Yes, but from whom, that's what I'm wondering," the girl replied darkly.

"We have to go to the meeting point," Anand said. "It's the only chance we have of finding Abhaydatta."

The banyan tree must have been hundreds of years old. Thick roots hung from its branches, and from them grew more banyan shoots, like green and brown pillars, forming a cool and shady hall of sorts in the middle of the noisy bus depot.

"Let's look around," Anand said. "There are a lot of travelers sitting around in the shade of the tree."

They searched methodically, walking in a spiral around the roots, moving closer to the center. They passed several sleeping men and a couple of families that were eating their lunches of flat brown bread, onions, and buttermilk—but no old man. Finally, they reached the original trunk, black with age and thick as a tower. At its foot someone had set up a deity, a small stone image of Ganesha, the elephant-headed god. It was garlanded with a cheerful yellow strand of marigolds.

"There's no one here," the girl said, her voice disappointed. "We should never have listened to that beggar woman. A liar and a cheat, that's what she was! She's probably laughing her head off right now, thinking of us standing here like fools. Now what will we do?"

Anand couldn't think of anything. The day had been

mercilessly bright and unusually hot for winter, not like the previous day at all. They had taken a bus to the Esplanade, but after that it had taken them a long time to find the meeting point. No one seemed to know where it was, not even when they mentioned the giant banyan tree. Almost as though it were invisible to ordinary folks, Anand thought, as he stared at the tangle of branches that extended in every direction. He was tired and sweaty and dispirited—and, he suddenly realized, very, very thirsty.

Someone had set up a big earthen pitcher of water and a dipper near Ganesha's statue.

"Let's drink some water," he said. "I'm so parched I can't even think straight."

There was a sign near the water. It said, BEFORE YOU DRINK, TRAVELER, YOU MUST WASH YOUR HANDS AND OFFER A PRAYER AND A FLOWER TO GANESHA, REMOVER OF OBSTACLES. Beside it sat a bowl of marigolds, somewhat wilted from the heat.

The girl grabbed the dipper and raised it to her lips. Anand, too, wanted a drink more than anything else. His throat was so dry that he could hardly swallow. But somehow he knew they must not ignore the sign. He pulled the dipper away from the girl's hand.

"Hey! What's wrong with you!" she cried, outraged. "What do you think you're doing?"

He pointed to the sign.

"Oh, that!" she scoffed. "I don't believe in such super-stition."

She grabbed for the dipper, but he quickly poured a lit-tle water over her hand and then his, and pressed a flower into her palm. She glared at him, but then she set the flower down at the foot of the image, just like he was doing. Anand tried to remember a prayer—his mother had taught him several. None would come to him, though. "Help us, please," he finally whispered to the portly statue, which seemed to have a kind and merry look in its eyes.

The two children drank deeply and washed their faces. The water was clean and refreshing as it dripped down Anand's neck. He wiped his face on the edge of his shirt, and when he looked up, there was the old man, sitting cross-legged, leaning comfortably against one of the banyan roots where Anand could have sworn no one had been even a moment ago. He looked exactly as he had when Anand saw him last.

"Abhaydatta!" the girl cried out excitedly.

Anand was so happy that he almost flung himself into the old man's arms. But he restrained himself. You didn't just go up and hug a Master Healer, particularly when you hardly knew him. Also, maybe Abhaydatta was displeased with him. First Anand had doubted him. Then he had overslept and been late. Then he had allowed himself to be tricked by Surabhanu. And perhaps—if the candy seller had really been the Master Healer in disguise—he had abandoned him to danger. "I'm terribly sorry," he started to say, guiltily, but Abhaydatta didn't let him continue.

"Certainly took you long enough, my boy," he said in a voice that wasn't the least angry. He spoke in a calm, unsurprised tone, as though they'd planned to meet at the banyan tree all along. Then he fixed his eyes on the girl. "I don't remember asking you to bring someone else along."

The girl looked at him with bold eyes. "It's not his fault. I made him bring me. I want to go with you, too. I'll be a good helper to you—better than him! If it wasn't for me, he wouldn't even be here. Go ahead—ask him."

Abhaydatta didn't ask. Anand had a feeling he knew exactly what the children had been through. It was even possible that he knew a lot more about them than they themselves did. He examined the girl for a long moment, a furrow between his eyes, until she dropped her head.

"Please take me with you," she said in a different voice, a pleading one this time. "I can't bear to go back to living under the soft-drink stall."

Abhaydatta sighed. "An even number is better than an odd one when starting on a journey like ours. But sometimes chance is a better guide than all the maps we construct. I'll take you, although I'm not sure I'm doing the right thing."

The girl clasped her hands tight and gave a skip of joy.

"You might not be so happy if you knew how dangerous our path is going to be. Things may go very wrong for you, perhaps for all of us, no matter how hard we try to safeguard ourselves."

"I don't care!" she said. "I want to go with you. I won't blame you no matter what happens to me."

"Very well," Abhaydatta said. "To another matter now. You seem to know my name. But tell me, what's yours?"

The girl hesitated, her face reddening. "I don't know," she said at last. "I was lost when I was little. . . ." To Anand's surprise, her voice quavered and she looked down.

"Tell me about it," Abhaydatta said gently.

"It was a long time ago. I don't remember it too well," the girl said. "I think my parents had brought me with them to see Kolkata, and somehow we got separated. There was a maidan crowded with lots and lots of people, and stalls selling balloons and roasted peanuts. Maybe it was a fair. I ran from stall to stall, crying and shouting for my parents, but I never found them."

How frightened she must have been, Anand thought with pity. "How terrible—" he started to say. But she gave him a glare and turned to Abhaydatta. When she spoke next, her voice was street hard and nonchalant.

"That's how I ended up living in the gap under the soft-drink stall. People have called me Sweeper Girl for as long as I can remember."

"That won't do anymore," Abhaydatta said with a smile. "Now that you are a member of our company, you require a suitable name. Come, you will choose one right now!"

He took out a sheet of paper from his bag and tore it in two. He wrote a name on each piece and folded it over, then held out the pieces to the girl.

"Choose whichever one you like," he said.

The hard look on the girl's face was replaced by one of excitement. She looked a bit scared, too. Anand could sense a little of what she was feeling. A new name was a chance at a new life, and not many people got that! Her hand trembled as she extended it to one paper, then the other, then snatched it back as though the papers were burning hot. As Anand watched, he saw that indeed one of the papers was on fire. But it was a strange kind of fire. It didn't burn the paper to ashes but only made it glow red, like lighted coals. The girl's hand was very close to it now. Why, she can't see the flames, he thought, and wanted to call out a warning. But even before he glanced at the still, intent look on Abhaydatta's face, he knew he must not. She had to choose her name on her own, even if the name she chose led her to misfortune. So he bit his lip and watched as her hand flitted back and forth between the two pieces of paper and finally settled on the fiery one. Abhaydatta let out a breath like a tiny sigh, but only Anand heard it because the girl was busy staring at the paper, trying to make out what it said. *Why*, Anand thought in surprise, *she can't read*. And then, *But of course. No one ever bothered to teach her.*

He craned his neck to look at the single word, scripted in looping Bengali letters. "It says Nisha," he said softly.

"*Nisha*! The night!" the girl exclaimed, looking up at him in delight. "I love it!" Dreamily, she added, "I've always liked watching the night sky, the way the faraway stars twinkle, beckoning to you, the way clouds move across Old Woman Moon's face. Sometimes when I couldn't sleep, I'd watch them from under the soft-drink shop. They always made my own troubles seem less important."

Anand stared at her. He hadn't expected the tough girl who'd guided him to the station to have a poetic side.

"The night is a time of great beauty," Abhaydatta said, "but also of danger." He put the other piece of paper carefully away in his bag, and for a moment Anand wondered what the other name he had offered the girl had been.

The girl didn't pay attention to the last part of Abhaydatta's statement. She flung herself at him and gave him a fierce hug, surprising both him and Anand. "Thank you! Thank you so much for giving me such a lovely name. How did you know to choose such a perfect one! I feel like a whole new person! I'll do anything for you, I will! And your eyes—I was right, they *are* just like my grandfather's!"

Abhaydatta smiled. "I hope the name will bring you luck, child," he said. "Now, it's time to go. Our bus is about to leave. We don't want to miss it, do we?"

Nisha clasped the old man's hand tightly in hers and walked next to him, chattering happily, as though the name-giving had formed a special bond between them. Feeling left out—and a bit envious—Anand followed behind. It was childish, he knew it, but he felt a sharp longing to hold Abhaydatta's hand, too. He watched the old man's profile thirstily. And thus when the old man turned his head, Anand saw what Nisha did not: The look on his face, even as he responded cheerfully to Nisha's chatter, was somber and sorrowful.

❧

Abhaydatta led them up to a green and white bus, a dusty, rickety vehicle with bundles strapped high on top.

"Wait, it says 'Allahabad' in front." Anand said. "I thought we were going to Pa—Pat—"

"Pathankot." Abhaydatta nodded. "We are. But we're going to take a couple of different buses to get there. It'll be safer that way. Now remember, you're my grandchildren, accompanying me to Allahabad, to bathe in the holy spot where the three sacred rivers meet. You must call me *Dadaji*, like local children would, and make sure you don't speak of anything concerning the real reason for our journey. One never knows who might be listening. I know you have a lot of questions, and I intend to answer as many of them as I can. But they'll have to wait until we're by ourselves again."

He hurried them up the steps of the bus, which was already crowded. In addition to human passengers, there were several chickens squawking madly from inside a sack, and Anand thought he heard, from somewhere in the back of the bus, the bleating of a goat. The three of them did manage to find seats, but not together. Two were on one bench, and the third was on the bench behind, where a fat, turbaned man had already occupied the window seat. Nisha pushed ahead and occupied the bench with two seats.

"Dadaji, Dadaji, come sit next to me," she called, beckoning to Abhaydatta, sounding exactly like a spoiled granddaughter. An annoyed Anand had to sit next to the turbaned man on the seat behind.

"This is the cheapest, and probably slowest, way to travel to Pathankot," Abhaydatta informed them as the bus started on its way with a rattle and a wheeze. "But it's also the safest."

It was also probably the most uncomfortable, Anand thought as the bus hit a pothole and bounced him hard against the worn wooden seat. Certain portions of his anatomy were sure to be black and blue by the time the journey was done.

"Our friend wouldn't be caught dead in here, among all the . . . *riffraff*, I think, is the term he likes to use," Abhaydatta added with a chuckle. "Let's hope he thinks that I wouldn't, either. Then we'll have a good chance of getting to Allahabad, and perhaps even farther, uneventfully."

ભ ૭

Abhaydatta was right. The day's journey was uneventful—if you called breaking down twice uneventful. Then there was the time when the engine overheated, and all the passengers who were carrying anything drinkable had to pour it into the radiator's steaming mouth. In between they stopped so the goat could be milked and the chickens (and the passengers) could get some fresh air. But the children didn't mind the interruptions or the discomforts of the journey.

"I don't remember ever being outside Kolkata before," Nisha said excitedly. "I never imagined there could be so much green anywhere!"

Anand, too, was fascinated by the world that sped by his window. He craned his neck around the fat man to watch tiny, picture-perfect villages with their thatched huts and mud walls, set in the middle of emerald rice fields. There were bamboo thickets and little ponds where women washed clothes. In places, they passed men in colorful turbans, riding on carts driven by huge buffaloes with painted horns. In places the rice fields gave way to tall fields of dark green stalks with long leaves that swished in the wind.

"What's that?" Anand asked.

"Sugarcane," Abhaydatta said.

"Sugarcane!" Anand said in wonder. "I've eaten it several times—my mother chops it up into pieces for a snack. But I never knew it grew this big. What fun it would be to own a whole field of it, to wander around it as you please, breaking off and chewing as many stalks as you want!"

All in all, it was a great day. Abhaydatta answered all their questions patiently, just as a fond grandfather would, and when the bus halted at a rest stop so that the passengers could stretch their legs, he said they could eat whatever they wanted from the vendors that had set up their wares.

"Can I have some of those alu pakoras?" Nisha asked, pointing to where a man was frying golden-brown balls of potato mix dipped in batter in a huge wok. "And maybe some roasted peanuts, and some yogurt, and some rasogollahs—I had one a long time ago. I love how sweet and spongy they are, oozing all that syrup—" She paused and looked at Abhaydatta worriedly. "Will that be too expensive?"

Abhaydatta smiled and ruffled her hair. "I have enough," he said. "As long as you promise not to get travel sick and throw up when the bus starts to move again."

"I never get sick!" Nisha said, outraged. "You know that, Dadaji!"

Anand watched her, impressed against his will. She sounded so natural—no one would have thought she wasn't related to the old man, that she had met him just that day. Not like Anand, who stumbled over his words each time he tried to address Abhaydatta as his grandfather.

"And what would you like?" Abhaydatta asked Anand. The look in his eyes was so kind that Anand felt better. He asked for some bread and potato curry. Abhaydatta bought some mangoes as well. "I think I know a young man who might like these," he joked. They carried the food—an immense quantity of it—to a cool spot under a tree. Abhaydatta beckoned to a man who was selling lassi, and the man poured them tall glasses of the frothy yogurt drink.

"Mmmm, delicious!" Nisha said. "I've never had lassi that tasted so good."

Anand silently agreed. A sleepy sense of well-being enveloped him. Perhaps it was the brave new landscape, hinting at many coming adventures. Or maybe it was the calm presence of Abhaydatta, solid as an ancient tree. In any case, Anand felt his earlier doubts leave him, along with much of his weariness. Even his muscles seemed to ache less. Trouble lay ahead, he knew that. But right now it didn't seem to matter. For the moment, he felt as though he was really off on a trip to bathe in the sacred river at Allahabad—and to have as much fun along the way as possible. He felt even better when he climbed back into the bus and discovered that the turbaned man had left, allowing him to have the window seat.

Nisha was dozing—no doubt the effect of the spectacularly large lunch she had eaten—and when Anand leaned forward, he saw that Abhaydatta, too, had his eyes closed. Anyone else would have thought that the old man was asleep, but Anand could tell he wasn't. There was an alertness to the way in which he held his body. Perhaps he was communicating with members of the Brotherhood? Anand hoped he would soon get a chance to ask him how one did that. Even more, he hoped that Abhaydatta would teach it to him.

Anand laid his head on the window and daydreamed about possessing telepathic powers. And who knew what else Abhaydatta might teach him! To transport himself to different times and ages using mind energy? (But perhaps Abhaydatta didn't know that, or else why would they be rattling along on this bus?) To change baser metals into gold? Ah, he could just see the look on his mother's face when he returned with an armload of shining nuggets. The late afternoon sun was warm on Anand's shoulders, and his eyelids grew heavy. He thought of his sister, how he'd buy her everything she'd ever wanted. He'd start with the princess doll. He remembered the one they'd seen in Laxmi Variety Store. Dressed in a red silk sari, it was slender and regal, with eyes that opened and closed and a mass of curly black hair on which sat a sparkling crown. Thinking of the doll, he fell into sleep.

He awoke with a crick in his neck and an uncomfortable feeling of being watched. He looked around at his fellow passengers, but they were all asleep. The sun was setting behind a long stand of trees—he didn't know their names. They'd traveled a long way now, and the vegetation was unfamiliar. There was a swatch of brilliant red in the sky that faded to orange as he watched. Against it a low, dark line of birds glided gracefully. Anand squinted to see better, but he couldn't tell what kind of birds they were. They were fast, though. Amazingly fast. They kept up with the bus quite easily—and they weren't even flapping their wings.

A vague uneasiness rose in Anand. He was probably being fanciful, but it seemed to him that the birds were going at exactly the same speed as the bus—as though they were keeping an eye on it. He looked over at Abhaydatta. This time, the old man was really asleep. Anand hated to disturb him. Who knew how little rest he'd had in the last few days, and how little he would get in the upcoming ones? But he saw that the birds had dropped lower. They were only a little higher than the roof of the bus now. They were a strange species—black as crows but much smaller, with beady orange eyes that glittered. Was it his imagination, or did he see one of them turn its head and focus those glittering eyes on the bus—and on him? An involuntary shiver came over him, and he moved away from the window and touched Abhaydatta on the shoulder.

Abhaydatta yawned and stretched like any ordinary man whose sleep has been disturbed. He didn't ask Anand why he had roused him. If he saw the birds, he gave no indication of it. Instead, he looked down at his hands and moved his lips silently, the way old men do, reciting their evening prayers.

After a minute he said, "I'm glad you woke me. I can never sleep at night if I've napped too long. Is there any water left in the bottle? A long bus ride really dries you out. Why, even my brain feels hot."

As he scrabbled under the seat for the water bottle, Anand dared to take a quick look outside. The birds had fallen behind and were no more than specks against the darkening sky. They disappeared even as he watched. He handed over the water bottle silently, wondering if the entire incident had been a product of his own overheated brain.

A CHANGE OF PLANS

With a jerk and a shudder, the bus stopped.

"Koila Ganj!" the ticket seller shouted, throwing open the creaky door.

Koila Ganj seemed to be a midsize factory town of little distinction that sat on a dusty plain in the middle of nowhere. Maybe, as its name suggested, coal was processed here. Peering from his window, Anand could see tall smokestacks lined up along the horizon, belching blackness into the sky. Even through the bus windows, the air smelled scorched and arid. Anand put the end of his shirt over his nose, hoping the bus would leave soon. There was something about the town he didn't like. Then, to his dismay, he saw Abhaydatta pick up his bag and beckon to them.

"I thought we were staying on the bus until it reached Allahabad," he said.

"Our plans have changed," the old man replied. He waited until they had walked away from the bus-stop crowd, then added, "Surabhanu is stronger than I realized, and he has many spies. I think I have deflected him for the moment, but staying too long in one place—even if it is a moving bus—may alert him to our presence. The two of you are particularly in danger of being found, because he has tasted the flavor of your energies."

Anand didn't like the sound of that. It reminded him all too clearly of the horrifying sensation in the train compartment, the invisible tentacle that had caressed his face.

"What are we going to do now?" Nisha asked. Her face was pale, as though she was remembering the same incident.

"Don't be afraid," Abhaydatta said gently to them. "Danger will come upon us when it will. We can't stop it. We can only try to be prepared. There's no point in looking ahead to that danger and suffering its effects even before it comes to us. Besides, as long as I am with you, I'll protect you with whatever power I have." He put his arms around both their shoulders, and at his touch Anand felt his heart lift a little. "Tonight we'll rest at an inn," Abhaydatta continued, "and enjoy as good a dinner as this town is able to provide, and tomorrow, when the sun is up and my mind is clearer, I'll know the best way to proceed."

Finding an inn proved to be more difficult than Anand had thought it would be. There weren't many such places in the little town—probably because travelers wisely gave it a wide berth, Anand thought. Finally, they came across an inn that looked fairly clean and new, on a noisy, lighted street near the marketplace, beside a toddy shop. Abhaydatta went up to the door and lifted the huge iron knocker. There were sounds of laughter inside, and merry voices singing a drinking song. But just as Anand was thinking how good his aching back would feel stretched out on a nice, firm bed, the old man released the knocker carefully and backed away.

"What's wrong?" Nisha asked, disappointed.

"There's a bad smell inside," Abhaydatta said with a frown.

"There's a bad smell everywhere!" Nisha burst out. But she knew, as did Anand, that the old man wasn't speaking of an ordinary odor.

They tramped down a street with an open sewer running alongside it, then another one, dimly lit, that led them to an older part of town. It was dark by now, and the roads were mostly empty. The few people they came across watched them unsmilingly, with narrowed eyes, as though they wished them ill. Finally, when Anand was certain he couldn't drag himself any farther, Abhaydatta stopped in front of an old mansion. Once it must have been a grand building, but now the paint had peeled off of it, and a couple of the shutters on the barred windows hung askew on loose hinges. A passerby would have had to look carefully to see the wrought-iron sign, rusted and half covered by creepers, that read YATRI HOUSE. There were no lights anywhere, and to Anand it seemed like the place was abandoned. But the old man rapped on the door and waited confidently.

"And this one is safer than the other inn?" Nisha asked, her voice skeptical.

"It's not what I would have liked, but yes, I think it is safer," the old man said, rapping again.

The door opened just a crack, and a gruff voice called, suspiciously, "Who's there? Back away! I have a stout stick here and am ready to use it!"

"Is this how you greet travelers who want to stay at your inn?" Abhaydatta answered mildly. "If so, I'm not surprised you don't have many customers."

"Why should you want to stay here?" The voice was still suspicious. "There are other inns in town, much fancier than mine. Didn't you see the one by the toddy shop? That's where they all like to go nowadays."

"Maybe there are still some who prefer a place that's owned by an honest man, even if it's not so fancy," Abhaydatta said.

The door opened a bit more. A middle-aged man who looked as though he hadn't shaved in days stood there, holding up a lantern. He looked guardedly into Abhaydatta's face, and then the children's, then waved them in and secured the door firmly behind them with a crossbar. "One can never be too careful these days," he mumbled. "There have been strange comings and goings."

"What comings and goings?" Abhaydatta asked, but the man shook his head and would say no more. He led them down an unlighted corridor and showed them to a room with three beds. Anand was surprised to see that the beds were high and ornately carved, with clawed feet. At one time, this must have been a very fine inn, indeed.

"I'll bring a broom and sweep it out for you," the innkeeper said, friendlier now, "and get you fresh sheets and blankets. There's a window you can open for fresh air, and a bath just down the corridor where the tap still works. I'm sorry I can't offer you more—business has fallen so much recently that I'm about to close down. This is one of the few rooms where I haven't sold the furniture yet."

"This suits us quite well," Abhaydatta said. "Could you get us dinner, too, my good man? My grandchildren and I are tired and would rather not go out again."

"Well, I've had to let the cook go, but I think I could fix you something simple myself," the innkeeper said. "You're right about not going out again, though. This town isn't as safe as it used to be." He left the lantern with them and shuffled away down the dark corridor, mumbling to himself.

"There's a strong bolt here, to keep intruders out," Anand said as he shut the door. He slid the bolt across and liked the definitive sound it made as it clicked loudly into place.

"That's good," Abhaydatta said. "Though the enemy I'm worried about cannot be kept out with an iron bolt. I'm more concerned about the window. No, not the one you're opening, Nisha, but that other one—" He pointed upward, and Anand saw that there was another tiny window—no more than two handspans across—near the ceiling. It was covered with chickenwire.

"Doesn't look like anything can get through that tiny opening," Nisha said doubtfully. "And anyway, it's covered with wire."

"Let's hope you're right," Abhaydatta said. "I just wish it had shutters that I could have closed and laid a stay-spell on."

Soon the innkeeper brought a meal of rice, eggplant curry, and yogurt to their room. It was simple but plentiful, and they ate it with relish. When they were done, Anand washed up and made for his bed. He was exhausted, and his eyes were closing already. Then behind him he heard Abhaydatta say, "Not yet, my child. Tired though you are, there are some things I must tell you both tonight. I don't know when we'll be in a secluded space again, where we can speak openly like this. Nor do I know how many more nights we'll be together. So the first thing we must plan is what to do if we are separated."

"But we won't get separated! Why should we?" Nisha demanded.

"If Surabhanu finds us, you must try to escape while I stay back and try to delay him."

"We won't leave you like that!" Anand cried. "We can't!"

The old man shook his head at Anand's protests. "You must. Remember, your allegiance is not to me, but to that which is greater than myself. And you are the Brotherhood's only hope."

Nisha listened intently to their conversation, her curious eyes moving from one face to the other. Anand could see she was dying to ask what they were talking about.

"If I am indeed overcome and cannot rejoin you," Abhaydatta continued, "you must go on alone to the Silver Valley. Look, I am going to draw you a map."

Abhaydatta knelt and drew a line on the cement floor with his forefinger. To Anand's amazement, the line began to glow at once.

"From Koila Ganj tomorrow we take the train. I hope to get to Ranipur, a small town in the foothills, by evening of the next day. We'll spend the night there, then rent donkeys and start climbing up these hill roads. There will be only a few small villages along the way—this road is little known and less traveled. The last of the villages is called Nag Champa. If we get separated along the way, wait here for me for a day and a night. If by then I cannot come, it will be because I am no longer able to."

Anand sucked in his breath, but the old man continued

calmly, "Then you must go on and not stop for any reason. Look here, past the village's northernmost boundary. There will be a rock here, shaped like a crouching dog. There may be snow at this height. There certainly will be later. I will need to buy you some warm clothes soon. Past the rock the foot road forks—take the left fork. You will come to a fast-flowing mountain river without a bridge. You must cross it."

"But—" Anand blurted, feeling inadequate. "I don't know how to swim. Do you, Nisha?"

Nisha shook her head.

"I cannot guide you on this," Abhaydatta said sadly. "The stream is not an ordinary one but the first obstacle on the path to the Silver Valley, created by the Brotherhood in the olden days. It appears differently to each person, based on his inner qualities. If you are a Being of Power, be it good or evil, you will be able to hear the voice of the river. Perhaps it will tell you how to ford it.

"Past the stream are two other obstacles. These, too, I cannot tell you much about. They have the ability to shift their shapes, to prevent travelers who may be dangerous to the valley from figuring them out. When the time comes, they will reveal themselves to you, and you will have to decide how to get past them. That will bring you to the pass that leads into the valley. When you see the three-pronged peak, you will know that you are there. Stand on the stone step in front of the peaks and call for the Healers. Someone will come to you.

"What's most important now," Abhaydatta added, "is that you commit this map to your memory. Look carefully at it again—I will draw it for you when we are in Ranipur, as soon as we are alone, and each night after that if I am still with you. Repeat to yourselves the directions I gave you. And now to bed! We have to make an early start tomorrow." The shimmery lines on the floor faded as he turned to Nisha. "Go and wash up, child. Here, take the lantern. We don't mind being in the dark for a few minutes."

Anand tried to grope his way to his bed, but he felt the old man's hand closing tightly on his arm. He was startled by how strong his grip was.

"Anand," the old man said in a low voice when he was sure they were alone, "there's one last thing. From here onward, I want you to carry the conch."

"What?" The surprise jolted Anand awake. He stared at Abhaydatta openmouthed. Abhaydatta delved into his bag and came up with a pouch with long fastenings attached to it. "I've put it in here. Tie this around your waist under your shirt—make sure it lies against your skin. Don't worry, it won't fall off—the conch has a will of its own, and one cannot lose it unless it intends to be lost. Remember, you must not take the conch out, no matter how great the danger you find yourself in. You must never try to use it. You are not trained to do so. To teach you even the basics of that would take a long time, much longer than we have—and it would be most dangerous for you."

Anand held the pouch in his hands for a moment, amazed again by how tiny the conch was, and how light. It pulsed in his grip like something alive. He was terrified by the responsibility, but also exhilarated. A great longing rose in him to look at it, just one more time. He pushed the thought away quickly. "Why are you giving me this?"

"Because I forsee danger. Surabhanu is near—I can sense him. He might strike at any time. Our one advantage is that he will focus on me, not you. He cannot imagine that I would hand over something as precious as the conch to someone else, least of all to someone who is not sworn into the Brotherhood. You see, when he embraced evil, he lost his understanding of what it is to trust. And this gives us a chance to save the conch and take it back to the Silver Valley."

Anand tied the pouch securely around his waist and covered it with his shirt. "Thank you for trusting me," he said. "I'll do my very best." But his heart beat unevenly. What if, when the time came, he failed the old man?

"You'll do fine," Abhaydatta said, as though he had read his thoughts. "You have the signs."

"Signs?"

But Abhaydatta would say no more. Instead he whispered, "There's one final thing: No one will notice that the conch is with you—not unless you tell him, or her. And you must never mention it to anyone. Not *anyone*. Do you understand?"

Anand peered through the half dark at Abhaydatta's face, which was suddenly more solemn than before, and felt an unpleasant sinking sensation in his stomach. "You mean Nisha, don't you?" he asked. "But why?"

The Healer started to say something, but there was no time. The light of the lantern was bobbing down the dark corridor toward them.

"I'm so tired, I could sleep for a year!" Nisha said with a huge yawn as she turned down the lantern's wick and flopped onto her bed.

Anand lay down and pulled the blanket up to his chin. The night was suddenly, unexpectedly cold, after the scorching day. Was there a smell of something new in the air, under the heavy factory-smoke stench, as though a storm was gathering in the distance? His mind was awhirl with all the things that had just happened. Why did Abhaydatta not trust Nisha? And the conch—was it truly with him? He touched the pouch at his waist and felt its small, hard outline. A shiver of excitement went through him. *I'm really a Conch Bearer!* he thought, and felt a grin split open on his face. But he was too tired to hold on even to this jubilant idea. The last thing he saw before he fell asleep was the silhouette of the old man against the shuttered window, weaving a closing spell with his fingers.

It is a dream he's having. Anand knows this because the colors around him are so much purer and more vibrant than they are in the waking world. The air of this dream world, too, is different. It is softer and lies like silk upon his skin, and smells of magnolias. And the view—it is more beautiful than anything he has ever imagined. He stands in a doorway, looking out at a beautiful beach of polished black sand that glistens in moonlight, bordered by a mysterious inky ocean in which silver waves rise and fall. The beach gives way to a thick forest on one side. It is an enchanted forest—Anand knows this instinctively— where magical beings are waiting to welcome him: unicorns, speaking birds, gnomes to play tag with him in clearings of four-leafed clovers, jinns to obey his slightest wish. He spreads his arms. In this world, he knows, it is possible to fly. But when he tries to launch himself out from his doorway into this spirit world, he cannot. Something is weighing him down, holding him back. He tries and tries, but the force is too strong. He twists and cries out in frustration, but to no avail.

Beneath a tree with heart-shaped leaves, a beautiful woman dressed in gauzy veils is standing. Did she just appear, or was she always there?

"Anand!" she calls, holding out her jeweled arms to him. "Come to us! We've been waiting so long for you."

"I can't move!" he shouts. "It's as though I have chains around my feet."

"It's the old man," she says in her low, musical voice. "He has you in his power and refuses to let you go. He wants to use you for his ends, and then, when he has achieved what he wants, he'll discard you like a mango that has been sucked dry. But we—we want you to stay with us forever, here in the moonlight forest where there is no sorrow."

Dejection sweeps over Anand as she speaks. She's right, the old man is cruel and uncaring. He's ready to deprive Anand of all this joy and endanger his life in the bargain. And for what? For something that Anand has been warned not even to look at, let alone use. Why should he follow such a hard master across the difficult wilderness and leave behind this sweet, enchanting world?

"Help me get away," he whispers to the woman.

"I can't." The woman's face is full of sorrow in the ethereal light. "He's too powerful. We spirit beings cannot cross the magic circle that he has constructed around the three of you. But you can help yourself."

She points behind him, and Anand turns in the doorway to look. Ahead of him is their room at the inn. In the small, feathery light from the lantern he sees Nisha and the old man lying fast asleep. They do not seem to breathe, and their faces are unattractive, the color of clay. He turns back and is struck once again by the perfect beauty of the world facing him. Why, this is the world whose existence he has always believed in, though until now he never had the opportunity to see it. Now that it is finally visible to him, he notices that it is exactly as he imagined it to be, only more beautiful. And the only thing that prevents him from stepping through the battered doorway of the old inn to this wondrous life is Abhaydatta. If he could just rid himself of the old man!

There is a clicking sound in his brain, as though a drawer has been shut carefully, and the solution is suddenly with him.

In the flickering light Anand picks up his pillow and begins to walk toward Abhaydatta. If he could just hold it down over the old man's face for a few minutes—that's all it would take! He wouldn't really hurt him. Of course not! He'd hold it there just long enough for the healer to become unconscious so that the bonds of his spell were loosened, allowing Anand to slip through them. He glances over his shoulder at the moonlit world for reassurance as he walks. Yes, it's still there, and the woman smiles encouragingly, her lips glistening red like pomegranate flowers, as though to say he's doing just the right thing. But in turning, he fails to see where he is going and stubs his toe hard on the clawed foot of his bed. It sends a bolt of pain up his leg. In angry surprise he thinks, *Dreams aren't supposed to hurt this much!*

That's when he realizes that he isn't dreaming. He's really standing there, his foot jangling with pain, a pillow in his hands, getting ready to kill a sleeping, defenseless man. That's how far the force has pushed him. The clever, insidious force that somehow wormed its way into him, that learned and used his secret longing to find a magical world to lure him this far. And if it can do that, what else might it be capable of? Certainly it can give him the physical strength to kill. He begins to shake as he realizes this, as he finds himself taking one step, and then another, toward Abhaydatta, unable to stop. He wants to say a word of power to halt his body, as the old man might have, but he doesn't know any. He tries to call out to Abhaydatta, but he's unable to make a single sound. He can't breathe.

What should he do? Thoughts fly past him like gossamer spores from a cotton tree, too fast for him to grab. But finally his mind latches on to one. *The conch!*

The old man had said he was not to use the conch under any circumstance. And yet, were there not emergencies so dire that they were exceptions? The conch, so close to him, so powerful, so filled with radiance, enough to lighten any heart, calm any mind—

With that thought a longing comes over Anand to hold the conch in his hands. *Just for a moment, just for comfort*, he says in his mind and realizes he's speaking to the conch.

He feels his right hand wrenching itself from the pillow. The pillowcase tears with a sound like a sigh. Anand sees his fingers are still clenched around it. He has to direct his attention to his fingers, to coax them open one by one. He places his splayed hand on his stomach, where the pouch hangs under his shirt, and feels his knees buckle, feels himself drop to the ground.

There's a different quality to the air in the room now—hard and bitter. He welcomes its unpleasant familiarity. He can hear his breath coming in harsh, ugly gasps, a sound so loud he wonders that the other two aren't wakened by it. The pillow has fallen from his hand. Slowly, reluctantly, he turns his head, but already he knows what he will see. The door has vanished. And even though he knows it was never really there, that it was merely the product of an evil conjuring, he feels tears of loss spring to his eyes. No, they are tears of fear: fear for himself, that he is so vulnerable to the dark manipulations of Surabhanu. Fear of what he might do the next time.

THE ONE-EYED DEER

"Get up, sleepyhead!" Nisha called, pulling at Anand's arm.

He came awake with a start. Sunlight flooded the room through the window, which was now wide open. The room looked bright and cheerful, and very ordinary.

"Dadaji is talking to the innkeeper. He wants us to leave soon—as soon as you're ready. Go and wash up, and I'll make the beds. He said we'll eat at the station, and catch an early train."

Anand stumbled to the bathroom, where he splashed cold water on his face. His head throbbed, and he felt tired and feverish. What a terrible dream he'd had last night. Even now, the feel of it made him shudder, though he couldn't remember the details too well.

They left for the station soon after. At the inn door, Abhaydatta put a thick wad of bills in the innkeeper's hand—far more than the man had asked for. The Master Healer seemed to have an unlimited supply of cash. Where did it come from? Anand wondered.

To the delighted man, Abhaydatta said, "This should help you get back into business. But mind, don't spend it all at once. You don't want people asking questions about where it came from."

As before, Nisha held on to Abhaydatta's hand and skipped ahead, chattering and pointing to things. Anand walked behind, grouchy and hungry, his head hurting. She was too darned cheerful, that girl, he thought. She'd really taken to the story the old man had created, about him being their grandfather. She kept calling him Dadaji, even when they were alone, and simpering up at him as she talked a mile a minute. So early in the morning, too! His own brain felt sluggish and exhausted. He tried to remember if he'd lain awake for a long while after that dream, afraid to sleep. But everything was hazy.

The station was a small one, just a ticket booth and a raised platform under some trees, but as always, there were food vendors. Abhaydatta stopped in front of one and bought freshly fried samosas stuffed with cauliflower to eat with a red chutney sauce. They smelled delicious, but Anand shook his head.

"I just want a glass of tea," he said.

"Are you feeling unwell?" the old man asked in concern. "You do look rather pale."

"I didn't sleep well," Anand muttered. "I had nightmares—"

"I'll say you did!" Nisha interrupted. "There was a big

chunk torn off your pillow when I made your bed this morning, as though you'd been fighting it. Did you think it was Surabhanu?" she giggled.

"Hush!" Abhaydatta said sternly. "Some things should not be joked about, and some names not spoken lightly."

But Anand hardly heard him. Nisha's words had hit him like a fist, bringing back the events of the night with knife-sharp clarity. How he'd found himself walking toward the old man, pillow clutched in his hands. How he couldn't stop his body from moving, no matter how hard he tried—not until he remembered the conch. He could see, for a moment, his fingers grasping the pillow. He heard again the fabric tearing with that sad, sighing sound. It was all real, then!

He followed his companions silently onto the train. Silently he sat staring out of the window as fields of golden mustard flowers and green maize flowed past them. He ate the lunch that Abhaydatta bought them. He answered the questions put to him automatically, listening with only one part of his brain. He even smiled at some of Nisha's jokes, though they weren't very funny. But all the time his mind was whirling, trying to come to terms with what he must do.

"Ranipur may be the best place to buy our warm clothes," Abhaydatta was saying.

"Oh Dadaji," Nisha cried, "can I have a red sweater? I've always wanted one."

"Yes," Abhaydatta smiled. Then he turned to Anand. "What do you want?"

"Anything will do," Anand said listlessly. He saw Abhaydatta give him a sharp glance. But Nisha was pulling at his arm.

"Dadaji, tell us a story."

Abhaydatta's eyes were still on Anand. He said, "Do you know the tale of the one-eyed deer?"

"No," Nisha said. "Don't you know stories about princesses? I really like stories about princesses, but a ghost story will do, too."

"First let me tell you this tale," Abhaydatta said. "It's an important one, and it may help you. There was once a deer that lived in a forest near a river. He was blind in one eye. While grazing on the grassy fields by the river, he was always careful to keep his good eye turned toward the forest, for he knew a fearsome tiger lived close by. At the slightest movement from the forest, he would bolt away. And thus he lived in safety for several years. But one day a hunter sailed down the river in a boat. The deer had never dreamed that danger might come to him from the river, and he was not looking in that direction."

"What happened then?" Nisha said.

"The hunter killed him," Abhaydatta said flatly.

"Oh, that's terrible!" Nisha said. "I don't like that story, Dadaji. Tell me another one."

"It's important that we don't act like the one-eyed

deer," Abhaydatta told her. But Anand felt that there was a special message in the story for him. Infected by Surabhanu, he was like the hunter, wasn't he, bringing danger to the company from the direction they least expected? He knew, then, what he would have to do, and what the result would be. The thought was like a deadly wound in his heart.

The two days on the train passed uneventfully, and in the evening they got off at Ranipur, a charming little town nestled in the foothills of the Himalayas, bordered by groves of pine and eucalyptus. This time, they didn't bother to look for an inn.

"It will be better for us if we are by ourselves," Abhaydatta said. But when Nisha asked him where they would stay, he smiled enigmatically and asked her to be patient.

Luckily, they had arrived on market day. The little open-air bazaar in the center of town, lit by strings of electric bulbs, was bustling with people. Bright woolen shawls hung festively from the eaves of clothing stores, and in the produce section apples and walnuts, brought in by farmers who lived in nearby villages, were piled in baskets. Open-air eateries offered roasted chicken and spicy naan breads cooked in open ovens. They stopped at one of these, and Abhaydatta asked for the best dishes the cook had to offer, but once again Anand only toyed with his food.

Abhaydatta bought coats for all of them, and woolen leggings, and caps that could be tied under their chins. He bought the children bags that they could sling over their shoulders and filled them with packets of walnuts and raisins, and sweets made from jaggery and sesame seed for energy—things that they could eat easily while walking. He also bought three wooden walking sticks, their ends reinforced with beaten metal.

"These will help us when we get to the snow line," he said.

"Snow!" Nisha exclaimed. "I've never seen snow, except in a calendar the soft-drink seller had tacked on the wall of his stall. Will we get to the snow line tomorrow?" Her eyes shone at the thought of all the adventures that lay ahead of them. But Anand kept his head low and plodded along behind. Not even the cream wool coat, embroidered with many-colored long-tailed birds, that Abhaydatta had chosen for him and arranged around his shoulders—easily the most beautiful thing he had ever possessed—could cheer him up.

They walked past the wooden cottages of the town along a path lined with fir trees. The path grew narrower and the trees taller as they left the town and its lights behind them. There was a quarter moon in the sky that provided them with some light, though once or twice they stumbled over rocks.

"Careful!" Abhaydatta said. "Don't stray from the

path. The hillside is steep here—if you fall, you might end up at the bottom of a ravine."

"Where are we going?" Nisha asked. "Is it far?"

"Not far now," Abhaydatta said.

"But we've left all the houses behind," Nisha said worriedly. "Are you sure this is the right way?"

The path had turned sharply and grown even narrower. The firs had given way to outcrops of rocks bordered by thick, prickly hedges. They had to follow the old man single file, and in one place, where the rocks squeezed close, and the hedges met above their heads, they had to double over. Even then, thorny branches pulled at their clothes and scratched their faces.

When they straightened up, Abhaydatta had vanished.

"Dadaji, where are you?" Nisha called. The dark mountains caught her voice and threw it back at them: *you, you, you.*

She shrank against Anand. "I'm scared! Where did he go?"

Anand was scared, too, though he tried not to show it. "He can't be far—he was here just a moment ago," he said. "Let's stay calm and look around." He parted the bushes around him, trying to see if the old man had tripped and fallen. But his mind was racing frantically. What if Abhaydatta had stumbled into a trap or been ambushed? What was he—they—going to do? What if the people who had taken him were waiting around the bend of the path for them? The moon had gone behind a cloud, and the black sky seemed low and threatening. He thought he heard a rustling behind him. He tried to remember the instructions Abhaydatta had given them in case they were separated, but in his fear he could recall nothing. There was that rustling again. Nisha gave a little shriek. With one hand he pushed her behind him and turned to face the sound. Instinctively, his other hand groped for the pouch that hung under his shirt.

Then, blessedly, he heard the old man's voice, speaking in a whisper. "I'm here." It came from a small gap in the hedge behind them. They struggled toward it and found that the gap led to a small opening in the rock. Abhaydatta was crouched there. He held a finger to his lips to signal them to be silent and beckoned to them to follow. He had something in his hands that produced a little light. Perhaps it was a flashlight, thought Anand, though he had not seen him buy one.

The narrow passage had now widened and grown taller, so they could stand. The light in the old man's hand grew stronger, and Anand could see they were inside a cave. It wasn't a bare cave, though. The floor was lined with sweet-smelling rushes, and there were blankets piled in a corner. Over to one side, there was a circle of stones where blackened remains of wood indicated that a fire had been lit before. And the walls—the walls of the cave were made of polished stone, and they glistened like black glass.

"Ah," Abhaydatta said with satisfaction as he looked around. "Here it is, just the way it is described in the Annals of the Brotherhood."

"You scared us, Dadaji!" Nisha complained. "You shouldn't have disappeared like that."

"It was a test," Abhaydatta said, "a very small one—to see what you would do if you found yourselves alone. Nisha my child, could you fetch me my bag from the corner?"

"And did we pass?" Anand asked angrily as Nisha went off to look for the bundle. He was surprised at how upset he was with the old man—now that he knew he was safe— for the trick he'd played on them.

"You didn't fail," Abhaydatta said cryptically. Then, in a low voice that was meant only for Anand, he said, "But you must rely more on your own intelligence—as all of us in the Brotherhood have been taught to do—and less on the magical. Magic is to be used only for high purposes, for things that impact the world. Or when there is no other recourse for our survival. You, particularly, must not turn to that which is forbidden to you. The conch will attract you. It will tempt you. It has great power, and that is the nature of power. But you must resist it. Remember, the conch could be as great a danger to you—in a different way—as Surabhanu." His eyes, as he looked at Anand, were so concerned that Anand felt his anger draining away.

"There's something I must tell you," he said. And

before he could change his mind, he blurted out to Abhaydatta what had happened the other night. Even when he noticed that Nisha had come back and was listening to his tale, he made himself continue, though humiliation burned his cheeks.

"I didn't want to tell you," he ended miserably, "because I was afraid you'd send me away. I tried to convince myself that it was just a dream. But it wasn't! Nisha saw the torn-up pillow. Somehow Surabhanu got to me and controlled my mind. Like the one-eyed deer, you watched out for danger from every other direction, but you trusted me—and it almost killed you. So now I must do what is right and go far from you, where I can't hurt you in any way."

"Oh, no, Anand!" Nisha cried, her eyes full of tears. "Where will you go?"

"I don't know," Anand said. "Home, I guess." He looked away because he didn't want her to see that his eyes, too, were filling with tears, and began to unfasten the pouch.

But Abhaydatta put out his hand and stopped him.

"You didn't give in to Surabhanu, though, did you?" he asked, eyebrows raised. "There was something in you that was strong enough to withstand his command."

"It wasn't me," Anand said, "it was the—" Then he saw Nisha's intent, listening face and broke off. "What if I'm not able to stop myself next time?" he asked.

"Now that we're warned of what Surabhanu might try, we'll set up our own defenses," the old man said. "No more talk of going away. I can't do without my assistants—both of them!"

"But—" Anand began.

"No more buts! Unless you're tired of journeying. Or perhaps you're afraid, and would rather go back to the safety of your home?"

"You know I wouldn't!" Anand said hotly. "I'm afraid, yes, but I want to stay with you and help you more than anything I've ever wanted in my life."

"More than *anything?*" the old man said musingly, almost to himself. "I think that, perhaps, you don't know yourself as well as you might, child." But then his eyes brightened and he clapped his hands. "To work, my assistants! I want you to gather me twigs from the mouth of the cave —enough to build a fire. We will need it to keep Surabhanu at bay tonight."

THE VOICE IN THE NIGHT

Soon the fire crackled merrily, bringing warmth and cheer into the cave. Anand held out his chilled hands to the flames and sighed with pleasure.

"Ah yes," Abhaydatta said. "A fire on a night like this is a blessing, isn't it? It will keep us comfortable, but that is not its main purpose. I will throw some herbs from the valley into the flames, and their fumes will protect us from all who intend to harm us. More herbs must be thrown in from time to time, for our enemy is strong and night is his special element. So it is important that we keep watch, taking turns all night, and keep the fire replenished."

"I'll keep watch first," Nisha volunteered. "I slept on the train—I'm not too tired."

"I must confess I am," Abhaydatta sighed, and indeed, in the firelight that danced over his features, he looked haggard. "I've been weaving spells around us ever since the birds appeared—no, Anand, you didn't just imagine that incident. Not that the spells have been wholly effective. Surabhanu was trained by the Brotherhood, after all, and knows many of the same ones. In any case, I'll feel better once I get a few hours of sleep. But first, the map again."

He moved the rushes aside, and with a few swift strokes, drew the way to the Silver Valley. He made the children trace the glowing lines with their fingers and recite the names, then made it all disappear with a snap of his fingers. "Bedtime now," he said. "Wake me whenever you get sleepy, Nisha. And remember, don't let the fire go out, for any reason."

"I won't!" Nisha said. They watched as Abhaydatta took a small metal container from his bag. Was there no end to the amazements that bag contained? Anand wondered. The Healer threw a small pinch of what looked like black grass into the flames. The cave filled immediately with a strong but not unpleasant smell. It was a salty, windy smell, unlike anything Anand had known before, but Nisha sniffed and said, "Why, it smells like the sea."

"Have you been to the sea then, my child?" Abhaydatta asked.

"I—I don't think so. I don't know why I said that—" Nisha stammered.

"It is possible your body remembers something out of your past that your mind has forgotten," Abhaydatta said. "Perhaps when we are in the valley I can help you—but this is not the time to think of such things. The name of this herb is, indeed, oceanweed, and although it grows in the snow, it carries many of the ocean's powers. It cleanses your thoughts, blowing away old, stagnant impressions. And just as an ocean protects a country's boundaries, oceanweed does the same with your mind."

With a reminder to Nisha to rouse him at once should anything strange occur, he lay down with his head on his bag. In a few minutes, he was fast asleep.

"What do you think Dadaji meant when he said he could help me?" Nisha whispered to Anand.

Anand, too, had been wondering about that. But he didn't feel like starting a conversation with Nisha. He still felt a prickle of annoyance at the easy intimacy with which she called the Healer dadaji. If she weren't here, he thought, I'd have the Healer all to myself. Then he pushed away the thought, ashamed, and said, grumpily, "I have to sleep—I'll have to keep watch later."

"Wait," Nisha persisted. "I've got to ask you a question. Why is that terrible Surabhanu after us? What does he want?"

Anand hesitated. One part of him felt that Nisha deserved an honest answer—after all, she was part of their fellowship and faced the dangers of their quest along with them. Already she had risked her life to warn him when he was trapped in the train with Surabhanu, for had he eaten the evil magician's food—he realized now—he would have been totally in his power. But another part of himself said, *Let her wonder! For once, you know something she doesn't, no matter how much she tries to toady up to Abhay-datta. Her precious Dadaji doesn't trust her—and I bet he has a good reason.*

Then he was ashamed all over again. What was happening to him? Where did these mean thoughts come from? He had always prided himself on being a decent chap. "You must ask the Healer tomorrow," he said, speaking as gently as he could.

But Nisha wasn't satisfied. "You know already, don't you?" she said in an outraged voice. "You both know, and you won't tell me. Is it because I'm a girl? Or is it because you think I can't keep a secret?"

Guiltily, Anand pulled his blanket over his head and pretended to sleep. But he could hear Nisha muttering angrily. Sentences came to his ears from time to time: *It's not fair! . . . Why should he trust you more than me? . . . I'm not the one who almost smothered him to death.*

Anand lay awake for a long time even after she fell silent. That last bit she had thrown at him, it still made him cringe. What if that evil urge came upon him again? he thought as he tossed and turned. If only he had the Master Healer's gift of easy sleep! But no, the rushes tickled his neck and made him want to sneeze. The floor of the cave was hard and uneven, and bits of sharp rock pushed through the rushes into his spine. He moved his body—surreptitiously, he didn't want Nisha to start in on him again—only to discover more sharp rocks. He could hear

Nisha walking around the room—trying to keep awake, he guessed. From time to time she kicked at a rock or a pile of rushes and muttered some more. I should have taken the early shift, he thought. But finally, he fell asleep.

. . . *and dreamed that someone was searching him. Hands moved over his body, looking for something, checking the pockets of his shirt, shaking out mounds in the blanket, patting his waistband. Were they a man's hands or a woman's? Or a girl's? He wanted to open his eyes, but they were heavy, as though drugged. But when the hands reached the pouch, he shook off sleep with the last bit of his strength and struggled up to a sitting position." Get away from me!" he croaked.*

"Ow!" someone said. "Waking you up is a dangerous task, young Anand! You have strong fists! I'm going to have a bruise the size of a pomelo on my arm!"

Anand's eyes flew open. Abhaydatta was kneeling next to him, massaging his arm with a rueful smile.

"I'm sorry!" he said, his face hot with embarrassment. "I had another dream—"

"Another dream!" Abhaydatta said, concerned. "I thought the herb would have kept bad dreams away. How is it—? No matter, the night is nearly done. Can you take over the last part of the watch? I've already put more herbs into the fire—you need only make sure that it doesn't go out. There's water in a pitcher in the corner—splash some on your face if you get too sleepy. Wake me at sunrise.

You'll see the light through the gap in the shrubs that cover the cave mouth."

Even before Anand could nod sleepily, Abhaydatta had drawn up the covers over his head.

It seemed to Anand that he had never felt so sleepy in his life. He washed his face, as Abhaydatta had suggested, and paced around as Nisha had done. He glanced at his two companions. They were deep in sleep, their bodies completely still. It was almost as though their spirits had left them and traveled somewhere far away. He shivered at the thought and told himself not to be fanciful. Still, he couldn't stop himself from feeling uncomfortably alone. The cave was silent except for his muffled footsteps on the rushes and the whispery sounds of the fire. The walls of the cave shone around him like dark glass, and in them Anand could see a hundred tiny reflected flames. When he stepped closer, he could see his own reflection in the polished stone—only it didn't look like him. The image was distorted, the mouth stretched out in a horrible grimace, while his hair stood up in two hard spikes on his head, like monstrous horns. He backed away from the wall in consternation. Would the dawn never come?

The reflections of the flames flickered around him eerily, tinged with a dark red that was different from the fire's orange color. It was the color of dried blood, of Surabhanu's gown. It sent a shiver up his spine, but he couldn't look away from it. And what was this? Each flame seemed to hold a face at its center. Anand rubbed at his eyes, knowing it couldn't be so. He was tired, and his mind was playing a trick on him. But when he looked again, there were the faces again. Actually, they were all the same face. His mother's! She was gazing at him with entreating, tear-filled eyes.

Anand backed away from the walls until he was at the mouth of the cave. A great sorrow weighed him down. His mother's face. How sad it looked, and how tired. She missed him terribly, he could see that. She was afraid for him, too, and wished he were with her. Life was harder for her now, without her son's help. After all, his sister was a just a child. How had he ever believed she could take his place?

A sob broke from Anand's throat. He'd made a great mistake in leaving her—he could see that now. His first duty was to take care of his mother and sister. Instead, he'd abandoned them to run after foolish dreams of adventure and magic. Who knew how they were faring now?

He became aware, all of a sudden, that a strong wind was blowing outside. When had it risen? It whistled and moaned and shook the shrubs that covered the cave mouth. He could hear branches scrabbling against the rock wall like desperate fingers. Then, beneath the moaning of the wind, he heard another sound—a voice.

"Anand, Anand," it called plaintively. "Where are you? I can't see anything—the wind's raised so much dust out here, and it's so dark!"

It was his mother's voice.

Anand knew it must be a trick, another way in which Surabhanu sought to entrap him. It was impossible for his mother to be here, on a windswept mountain path hundreds of miles from Kolkata.

"She's safe asleep in her bed," he said determinedly and put his hands over his ears. "It's just an illusion."

Still, he heard the voice.

"I'm scared. Where are you? Come to me, son." It broke a little on the last word, and then he was listening to his mother sobbing. His brave mother, who took such good care of him always, who worked so hard after Father went away. How many times had she stayed up with him when he was sick, even if she had to go to work really early the next day! How many times had she divided up whatever little food there was in the house between her children, pretending that she had eaten already! His mother, who rarely ever cried.

What if Surabhanu had somehow found her and brought her here with his power to punish Anand for disobeying him?

"Anand! Anand!" the voice called, fainter now. It sounded as though his mother was wandering away from the cave into the darkness of the hillside. What if she stumbled in the dark? What if she fell down one of those sheer rock faces Abhaydatta had warned them of earlier? An image rose in Anand's mind, horrifyingly clear: his mother's body, twisted in a heap at the bottom of a ravine. With a cry he pushed his way into the thorny branches that guarded the cave mouth.

He had stiffened his body, expecting his skin to be torn raw by the sharp branches, but what he encountered was quite different. It felt to him as though he had walked into an invisible rubber wall. It gave a little as he pushed against it, but he couldn't get through. Abhaydatta must have laid a protection spell on the cave opening.

"Anand!" his mother called. She sounded exhausted. "I can't see the path. I—" She broke off with a cry, as though she had stumbled. Did she fall down? Anand held his breath, but the voice said nothing more.

"Mother!" he cried as loudly as he could. "Don't move! I'm coming!" He held her image firmly in his mind as though that would keep her safe and jabbed his hands into the rubbery air.

"Let me through!" he cried with fierce desperation.

He felt the invisible wall melting, falling away. Now thorny branches were raking his skin. He forced them apart with all the strength in his arms.

"Mother!" he yelled. "Don't worry! I'll find you!"

But if it were indeed his mother out there, she didn't hear him, because right then the wind rose in a roar. It formed itself into a huge funnel of dust, like a tornado, and rushed into the cave through the opening Anand had made in the branches. The force of its passing flung Anand onto the cave floor. Even as he realized what a terrible mistake he had made, the breath was knocked out of him. He couldn't even shout out a warning to Abhaydatta.

The fire went out.

The wind was so strong that Anand couldn't stand up. He did his best to crawl toward the spot where Abhaydatta had been sleeping, but in the dark he had lost his sense of direction. No matter which way he went, he ended up against a cave wall. He could hear, through the roaring of the wind, sounds of struggle. A man yelled something, there was a sound of metal ringing, like sword on sword, and then a bloodcurdling scream—a thin, high sound such as a wild animal might make, dying.

"Abhaydatta!" Anand shouted desperately. "Nisha! Where are you?" But his voice could not be heard above the din. He tried to make his way to the center of the funneled fury of wind, but he couldn't even get close to it. In his fear and frustration, he pressed his hand against the pouch. He could feel the conch in there. Even through the cloth, he could tell that it was hot.

"No!" Anand said to himself. He'd already fallen prey to Surabhanu's trickery and made it possible for him to enter the cave. If he took out the conch now, Surabhanu would feel its presence immediately. He would wrest it away, and Anand would not have the strength to stop him.

But the need to take the conch out was impossible to control—like the shivering that ran through a patient suffering from malarial fever. Anand could feel it taking over his body. His fingers moved of their own will to the pouch's mouth. Another minute and the conch would be in the open.

Anand closed his eyes, and through the frightening din around him, he focused on the conch as he had seen it that first night, in his shack in the Kolkata slums. He called up the powerful unearthly glow that had come from its small, flowery shape and was amazed at the rush of love and reverence that overtook him.

"Help me," he whispered. "I can't stop myself by myself."

The wind was deafening, but he could have sworn that through it he heard a small, clear voice say, "Ah, I've been waiting for you to ask."

And immediately he felt he was in the center of a bubble of stillness. Something important was happening, something that had to do with the conch. Had it really spoken back to him? The thought swirled away from him, and in its place a great music rose up. He wasn't sure if this music was outside him or in his mind. It was sweet like a mountain spring, yet grand like the melody the stars make as they travel the firmament. He felt his hand tremble, then fall back to his side. The wind was rushing from the cave now, as though it were being sucked away. It tore through the branches at the cave mouth, snapping them viciously as it went. Anand tried to stand up, but he couldn't. His legs were shaking too much. However, the cave was no longer as dark as before. As he stared, the first light of dawn filtered into it past the broken, ruined branches.

Anand could see Nisha on the other side of the cave. She was sitting with the blanket drawn tight around her, not moving, her eyes large and terrified. Ashes from the dead fire were scattered all around her. There was no sign of Abhaydatta.

THE FIRST OBSTACLE

Anand wasn't sure how long he crouched in a corner of the cave. Without Abhaydatta, the cave had suddenly become a dreary place, cold, and empty as a husk. Its walls, where Anand had seen his mother's face so vividly in its sorrow, were dull and opaque now. With all his being, he wanted to get away from the cave, from the painful memories and the shame of having done that which he had most dreaded. But he lacked even the will— or the strength—to make it across the expanse of the stony floor to where Nisha was sitting, arms wrapped tightly around herself, rocking a little. Once in a while, she moaned.

Anand wanted to moan, too. No, he wanted to weep and beat his head against the hard floor of the cave until the blood came. The pain would be a welcome one. It was the least he deserved for his betrayal—unintended though it was—of the Master Healer. But he knew he could not afford the luxury of guilt, or grief, right now. Surabhanu, not finding the conch on Abhaydatta, would surely return to the cave. And as Abhaydatta had said, Anand's first duty was to the conch.

He knew that his only hope—and Nisha's— lay in getting away from the cave as quickly as they could. Perhaps if they managed to cross the river, the first obstacle that Abhaydatta had spoken of, it would give them a little time and some protection from Surabhanu.

He dragged himself to his feet and walked shakily over to Nisha.

"We've got to go," he told her. But she didn't look at him. She kept rocking and moaning. He could make out the words she was repeating: *Dadaji, Dadaji.*

Guilt made his voice harsher than he intended. "Come on!" he cried. "We don't have time for this now. We've got to go."

"I saw the wind rushing in," Nisha said. "It had the face of a wild boar. Before Dadaji could wake up, it grabbed him in its teeth."

"What happened then?" Anand couldn't stop himself from asking.

"I couldn't see any more—it was like he was sucked into a giant funnel." Nisha started crying. "I should have helped him, tried to pull him away, but I was too scared."

Anand wanted to comfort her, but he didn't know how. He placed a hand awkwardly on her shoulder, but she shook it off. "It's all your fault! It was your watch. You should have seen the danger coming and warned Dadaji in time."

Anand cringed inside. It *was* his fault—far more than Nisha guessed. A part of him wanted to confess to her and lighten the burden on his heart. But another part knew nothing would be gained by it. She would blame him, perhaps hate him. And right now they needed to believe in and support each other. Because the two of them were all they had.

"It's not safe here," he said, speaking as gently as he could. "Let's try to get to the river."

"I don't want to anymore, not without Dadaji. What use is it? We'll never make it to the hidden valley without him to guide us, anyway. And even if we did, why would they let us in? You go if you want to. I'm staying right here."

Anand was tempted to take Nisha at her word. Every time he looked at her swollen eyes, guilt twisted inside of him. It would be a relief to be free of her! He didn't mind solitude—he was used to not having friends.

But he couldn't leave her in the cave to face Surabhanu by herself. That would make him a worse traitor than he already was.

"It's not safe for you here," he repeated.

"Why not? Now that he has Dadaji, why would that Surabhanu bother with me—or you?"

Anand swallowed. He knew he'd have to tell Nisha about the conch. There was no way around it. "Abhaydatta was taking something special back to the Brotherhood—

something that Surabhanu had stolen from them. Surabhanu came after him to get it back. But . . . he didn't get it."

"How do you know?"

"Because Abhaydatta gave it to me to carry."

"And you never told me all this time!" Nisha cried. "Me, who saved your life!"

"I'm sorry," Anand said. "I couldn't—I'd promised him not to let anyone know. But I had to tell you now, so you'll know the danger we're in. That's why we must hurry, and be more careful than ever before."

"This thing . . . what is it? I want to see it!" Nisha spoke emphatically.

"I can't show it to you. It's not safe."

"Nothing's safe, according to you! How can this make things worse?"

"Surabhanu will sense its presence."

"I'm not moving a single step unless you show it to me," Nisha said in her most stubborn voice. "You owe me this much at least, after having lied to me—"

"I never lied—" Anand began hotly. But then he stopped. Keeping a secret from a friend was a kind of betrayal, a kind of lie. And to make it worse, he'd reveled in his knowledge, proud of being the one Abhaydatta chose and swore to secrecy.

But did he dare go against Abhaydatta's explicit command and show the conch to Nisha? The Master Healer had underlined the danger of such an act. And yet Anand's only other choice was to leave Nisha behind. He could tell by the downturn of her lips that she wouldn't come with him otherwise. And how could he do that, leaving her to be destroyed by Surabhanu's wrath when he came back to the cave to discover that the conch had slipped from his grasp once more.

What shall I do? he asked himself in silent distress. No answers came. He closed his eyes and thought of Abhaydatta, that serene face, those kind eyes. Still, there was nothing. Wherever the old man was—if he was alive at all—he was unable to send a guiding thought back to Anand.

Then there was the feeling of music inside him again, but very soft this time, like the thinnest lute strings vibrating against his ribs. And a voice that was not a voice said, "You humans fret so much over little things. Always swinging between elation and despair. I thank the Great Power that I don't have to contend with emotion!"

Anand felt as though a surge of electricity had coursed down his back. The conch was speaking to him again—and on its own this time, even before he asked it a question. He held his breath at the impossible wonder of it. Abhaydatta hadn't ever indicated that such a thing might happen. The conch was speaking to him, Anand, the idiot taken in by Surabhanu's trick, the fool who endangered their fellowship by his wrong action! He didn't understand why it should be so, but he accepted the blessing humbly. It made the sting inside his heart a little less.

"Go ahead," the voice said. "It's all right. You can show me to Miss Mule Head. It's clear she won't budge until you do so."

Anand hid his smile at the conch's description of Nisha and reached underneath his shirt. As always, the touch of the conch sent a comforting warmth through him—but also a shiver. There was power here, power more complicated than he could even begin to understand. It had saved him a while back, but it could just as easily destroy. No one had told him this, but he knew it as a certainty in some deep, wordless part of himself. He curled his fingers around the conch and brought it out into the miserable dimness of the cave, squinting to shield his eyes from its blaze. But this time it only gave out a reassuring glow, like a candle in a fog. It was a balm to his eyes.

But Nisha wrinkled her nose. "That? That broken, muddy piece of shell? You must be joking!" When he shook his head, she sighed and said plaintively, "I don't understand. I wish Dadaji were here to explain it to me." After a minute, she turned away to gather her few belongings, her shoulders slumping dejectedly. Anand tucked the conch back into the pouch. He was thankful that she couldn't see the conch's beauty, but also sad for her. And like her, he wished Abhaydatta were with them.

They shouldered their bags and rolled up the blankets

they had slept in. They would need them—the next few nights would be cold. They would be climbing to the snow line soon, and perhaps be forced to sleep in the open. He followed Nisha to the opening of the cave, bending low to pass through it. It seemed smaller than before, as though the cave was shrinking. Was this, too, because of Abhaydatta's absence? Had he, with his powers, made it a place other than what it really was? Would it disappear totally when the spell wore off? And the Healer—where was he now, and what was happening to him?

Anand shook his head, which ached under the press of all the thoughts that crowded and confused it. I must focus only on the task ahead, he thought. That is what Abhaydatta would want of me. He wished he could better recall the map the Healer had drawn for them, but its outlines seemed very vague.

It was then that Anand saw the rag lying twisted in a corner. He had almost passed it by when he decided to take a closer look. His heart sped up as he realized what it was. Abhaydatta's bag, empty and crumpled now. Sorrow stabbed his heart again as he picked it up, so pitifully light. He wanted to throw it away—it was too painful to hold it in his hands and remember the man he had grown to love so quickly and deeply. But finally he folded it and slipped it inside his own bag. How many times had Abhaydatta touched that bag, drawing from it one small marvel or another! How he had delighted in astonishing

Anand and Nisha with those marvels. For the sake of those times, Anand decided, he would keep the bag with him, though it was of no use.

Anand and Nisha argued about the way they should take, drawing and redrawing the map with sticks on the frozen ground. Neither of them, he discovered to his dismay, remembered it fully. Once, mentally, Anand called to the conch to help them, but there was a pointed, though not unsympathetic, silence. Perhaps there were some challenges that the children were required to meet on their own. The ways of the conch were mysterious, and as he trudged back from one more trail that dead-ended in solid rock, Anand wondered if even a lifetime would be enough for him to learn them.

But finally, after several attempts, they found a twisting track that led them upward. It was slippery with slush; the two had to use their walking sticks to keep themselves from sliding backward. From time to time they would see a grove of stunted apple trees with wizened fruits, or a hut with a thin thread of smoke rising from its chimney. Sometimes there would be a couple of children foraging for twigs or leading a herd of long-haired goats to graze on a patch of green. Anand watched them at their ordinary tasks with a sense of longing that surprised him. Why should you miss such mundane things, he chided himself sternly, when all these years you wanted more than anything else to escape from them into the world of magic and high adventure? But the ache remained. Once he saw a boy and girl—brother and sister, he guessed—walking along the trail, their backs bent under baskets of dried grass. Meera's face came to him all of a sudden, earnest and happy and anxious all at once, the way it had been on the morning he had left home. Why, he had hardly given her a moment's thought since then! He waved to the boy and girl, wanting to share his walnuts and raisins with them, but to his dismay they ducked away with fearful looks and would not return his greeting. It was as though they knew, intuitively, that there was something perilous about Anand and Nisha, something they had better stay away from.

They looked for the village of Nag Champa all day, but did not find it. This worried them, and also the fact that the terrain looked very different from what Abhaydatta had described. Was it because of the snow that shrouded outlines and covered up landmarks, or was it some other enchantment?

It had started snowing late in the afternoon, and in spite of his coat and sturdy shoes, and the blanket he had wrapped around himself, Anand was miserably cold. Nisha shivered and blew on her hands from time to time. They were tired, too, and longed for something warm to eat. Though they passed a hut or two along the way, there were no signs of any inhabitants of whom they might buy food with the few rupees Anand had left. It was as though the snow had put all life on the planet to sleep.

Anand walked on doggedly, with his head low, but his mind swirled with doubts. Perhaps they were on the wrong path. Perhaps Nag Champa and the river were somewhere far away by now. He wasn't sure how they would survive in the snow, and whether, if things became really dangerous, the conch would help them. It frustrated him that he could not figure out the mysterious laws by which the conch operated. Still, at the thought of the conch, a small flower of warmth bloomed in him.

"Look!" Nisha was pulling at his arm, pointing westward. "Doesn't that look like a crouching dog?"

Anand turned his head. The snow was falling fast and thick, and wet flakes clung to his lashes. He brushed them away and squinted. "Could be," he said doubtfully.

"I'm positive it is!" Nisha cried excitedly. "See, there's the snout, the tail, the two forelegs. Come on, let's see if there's a river beyond it!"

They hurried through the slush that pulled at their ankles. Indeed, beyond the lump of rock that didn't look like much of anything to Anand, there was a river—a good-sized one. A white surge of water rushed down a steep bed studded with rocks. The noise was deafening. How was it that they hadn't heard it earlier?

"This is it!" Nisha said. "Let's try to cross." She rolled

up her leggings and took off her shoes and tied them around her waist. She dipped a foot gingerly into the water and jerked it back out. "Oof! It's *cold*!" she said.

Anand stared at the water. The river, even if it had been an ordinary one, would be hard to cross. Chunks of ice flowed down it, crashing against rocks and exploding into pieces. Inexplicably, it hadn't frozen over. He couldn't tell how deep it was—the foam swirled so much—but he had a feeling that it wasn't going to be shallow. Was it his imagination, or had the spate of water increased even as he stood here?

"If it is really the magic river, the first obstacle, we can't just cross it," he said to Nisha. "Abhaydatta told us to listen for it to tell us what to do."

The two of them stood by the bank for a few minutes.

"I'm listening hard," Nisha said. "I don't hear anything except water. Do you?"

Anand shook his head miserably. After the conch had spoken to him, he had hoped, secretly, that his special power was to hear things that others did not have the ability to hear. But it seemed not to be so.

"We've got to give it a try," Nisha said. "The light is going. Any darker and we won't be able to see even our own legs. I'd feel a bit safer on the other side, wouldn't you?"

She stepped into the water, flinching from the cold but determined. She took a step, then another. "It isn't too deep here—there are rocks underneath," she called over her shoulder to Anand. "I think we can get across if we're careful." She felt around with her stick to see if there was another rock she might step on. But the stick went down all the way, and would not come up again when she pulled at it.

"It's caught!" she exclaimed, annoyed, and gave it a great yank. But instead of coming up, it went down farther with a jerking motion—almost as though someone else had taken hold of the other end and were pulling it deeper into the river, Anand thought. Nisha lost her balance and fell in.

When she came to her feet, struggling and gasping, the water was up around her armpits. "Something's got my leg," she cried, her face white. "It's like teeth!"

"You must be caught between two rocks," Anand said. He kicked off his shoes and stepped in to free her. The icy water sent a shock through his body.

"No—not rocks! It's pulling me away," Nisha shouted. "Help!" And indeed the current—or something else—was moving her away from Anand. She flailed around, terrified. Her bag fell from her shoulder and spun away in the current. Anand reached for her hand, missed, and fell in face first. The water was deathly cold. It almost blinded him, but he thought he saw, for just a moment, something coiling and uncoiling down there in the current. Something huge, because he couldn't see where it began or ended. Something with tentacles—or were they mouths? He broke through the water, gasping, and found that Nisha was almost beyond his reach. He waded in as far as he dared and thrust his walking stick at her.

"Grab it!" he shouted.

For a moment he thought she wouldn't be able to, but somehow she managed to grasp its end and hold on. He pulled her toward the bank. It was slow-going, but surprisingly, it wasn't as difficult as he thought it would be. Soon he had her on dry ground—if the bank, knee-deep in snow now, could be called dry ground! She coughed and sputtered, and her lips were blue with cold and shock, but otherwise she seemed all right.

Then he looked at her leg and gasped. There were two semicircles of red indentations on either side of the leg, at calf-level. They did, indeed, look like teeth marks. From giant teeth.

"Thank God it's not bleeding!" he said.

Nisha shook her head, looking confused. "Whatever it was, it was certainly strong enough to have bitten off my whole leg—I don't know why it didn't. And the strangest thing was that as soon as I grabbed your stick, it let me go."

Anand didn't say anything. He was wondering why the water creature hadn't come after him with one of its other mouths. Was it because he carried the conch? Had the creature—possibly a guardian placed in the river by the Brotherhood—recognized the conch when Anand fell into the water? Would it allow them to pass if Anand went first?

"We've got to try one more time," he said.

"Are you crazy?" Nisha said through chattering teeth. "That thing's still down there. I'm not going in, not for a hundred magical valleys!"

"This time, I'll go first," Anand said. "If I seem to be doing all right, you can follow me."

Anand stepped into the icy rush of water. No creature came at him, so he gingerly took another step, then another. The current was very strong. It tugged insistently at his legs. Was the roaring of the river even louder? He could hear Nisha yelling something at him from the bank, but even when he turned, he couldn't make out her words. He looked upriver, in the direction she was pointing, and saw a huge spate of water cresting toward him like a tidal wave, glittering in the last light with a host of ice shards. It was too close—he'd never make it back to shore before it hit him.

He was right. Even as he struggled toward the bank, the giant wave hit him. It swept him off his feet and buffeted him around, but did not carry him away as he had feared. After a minute or so, its surge passed and he was able to struggle ashore. Nisha ran to give him a hand, and watched with concern as, coughing and choking, his mouth filled with river gravel, he collapsed on the bank.

"Are you all right?" she asked, thumping him on his

back. "It really scared me when I saw the wave coming. I thought you were going to die, for sure." Her voice wobbled a little. "Did you see? There were ice pieces in it, like spears." Then she recovered herself and said sternly, "I told you it was a stupid idea."

Anand smiled waveringly, but he was thinking about something else. Clearly, the river had chosen not to kill him, as it might so easily have done. But it would not allow him to pass even though he was the Conch Bearer. And for some unfathomable reason, the conch would not—or could not—help him. He remembered Abhaydatta saying that only a Being of Power could ford the river. He knelt on the frozen ground as the last light faded and couldn't keep his eyes from filling with tears. All this time he had hoped, silently, that he was such a being. But he wasn't. He was just an ordinary boy who couldn't make it past even the first obstacle the Healers had set on the way to the hidden valley.

MORE NIGHT VISITORS

They decided to shelter in the shallow crevice between the forelegs of the dog-shaped rock. It wasn't much of a shelter. The snow had stopped, but the wind whistled its way into the crevice with a chill that struck at the bone. The children's clothes were soaked through, and even their blankets were wet. In addition, Nisha had lost her bag with all her supplies.

"Don't worry," Anand consoled her. "Abhaydatta gave me a lot of food—it's a bit wet, but otherwise it's fine. There's enough for us both, for several meals."

"I'm not worried about starving," Nisha said testily, her teeth chattering. "I'm quite certain we're going to freeze to death long before that!"

Anand grinned at her tone, glad that she had recovered from the shock of the incident at the river, but he knew she was right. It was too cold for them to last even one night out here. He looked around him, wondering what he could do. The walls of the crevice were lined with what looked like dry, dead moss. If only he had matches, or a flint, he could have scraped them off and started a fire. He rummaged through his bag, hoping he had missed something that Abhaydatta had slipped in there. But there were only a few packets of food. And the folded bag that had belonged to the Healer.

Anand took out the bag. Perhaps he could give it to Nisha to wipe her hair. She had sneezed twice already, which worried him. The bag was lumpy in his hand. And wasn't it a little heavier than before? He put his hand inside, though he knew it was empty. When his fingers closed around something, he was surprised, but not entirely so. In the world he had inhabited ever since he met Abhaydatta, anything could happen.

"But they don't happen by chance," a voice said inside his head. It was a voice he was learning to recognize, but each time it appeared, it sent a thrill of excitement through him. "Did you think one finds a Master Healer's bag just by chance?"

"Conch!" Anand whispered, his heart filled with gladness. He glanced at Nisha, but she didn't seem to have heard anything. In his head he asked, "But why don't you answer sometimes when I need help?"

"As you have guessed," the conch said in its calm voice, "some things belong to the realm of humans. There, you must ask other humans for help—or, better still, help yourself."

"But how will I know which is which?"

"You'll learn."

If Nisha could hear this conversation, Anand thought, she'd probably say, "I'm heartened that you think I'll have time to learn anything before I freeze to death."

He heard the smallest chuckle inside his head. Why, the conch could hear his thoughts! Even those not addressed to it! Anand was taken aback by this. It was a little daunting to realize that someone was able to read everything that was in his mind. But on the whole he liked it. It gave him a strange but comforting sense of not being alone.

"Why don't you take a look at what you found inside the bag?" the conch was saying.

Anand brought his hand out. It held a box of matches!

"Did you think your Master Healer would bring you this far only to abandon you?"

"No! Of course he wouldn't!" Anand said, his heart beating madly with joy and excitement. "Is he alive, then? Where is he? Oh, how I wish he were here with us!"

But the conch would say no more.

"What are you muttering to yourself?" Nisha asked.

"I've found some matches!" Anand said. "Help me pull down some of this moss, and we'll light a fire."

"About time!" Nisha said, and she started tearing at the moss with enthusiasm.

Soon they had a small but sturdy fire going at the mouth of the crevice. They held out their hands to it, marveling at how much warmth—and cheer—its small flames generated. In a little while, their clothing was almost dry. They shared a packet of nuts and raisins, then rolled themselves up in the blankets, ready to sleep.

Suddenly Nisha exclaimed, "What's that?"

Just beyond the fire, Anand could see a pair of glowing eyes. Looking closer, he saw that they belonged to a small animal—something like a squirrel, except that its tail was longer and very bushy. The animal chittered at them, seemingly unafraid.

"Oh, look, isn't it cute!" Nisha said. "I bet it's cold and wants to get in here." A thought struck her, and she turned to Anand in consternation. "Perhaps this hollow is where it lives, poor creature, and we just took it over! We must let it in."

Anand watched the squirrel creature with suspicion. It didn't look dangerous, but it didn't look like an ordinary animal either. For one thing, Anand hadn't seen any wildlife since they had crossed the snow line. For another, it was strange that a wild creature should be so unafraid of them—and of the fire.

"There's something not quite right here," he said to Nisha. "I don't think we should have anything to do with that animal."

But Nisha had already reached her hand out past the fire. The creature sniffed at it, then put out a paw to touch her fingers.

"Oh, look, it likes me." Nisha smiled. "Isn't it amazing how friendly it is?"

"Yes," Anand said, chewing his lip. "It's quite amazing."

"Come here, little fellow," Nisha called.

"Don't!" Anand started to say. "What if it's not a real animal. . . ." But the words sounded foolish even to his own ears, and he let them trail away.

The creature scampered in and when Nisha extended her arms to it, it climbed into them. It was a handsome animal, whatever it was, Anand admitted grudgingly. Its fur was shiny and golden, tinged with red, and its eyes, too, were golden. There was a smudge of black between its eyes, like a wrinkle, which made it look as if it were deep in thought. It watched Anand unblinkingly, almost as though it was trying to tell him something.

The shock of being dunked in that cold river is getting to me, Anand thought. He wrapped himself tightly in his blanket and said a brusque good night to Nisha. He could hear her talking to the squirrel creature in the high voice people reserved for babies.

"Would little Rajah like some nuts?"

What! She was wasting their meager rations on that long-tailed rat! And she called it Rajah!

If that creature's a king, then I'm a Master Healer, Anand thought grumpily.

"Come, Rajah, let's cuddle up," Nisha was saying.

When the animal rubbed its head against her cheek, a smile broke across her face.

Anand wanted to warn her that it probably had fleas, but he bit his lip and remained silent. She must be feeling lonely and scared, just as he was, and disheartened at being defeated by the river. If the squirrel makes her happy, he thought, why not? And with that he fell into an exhausted sleep.

ॐ

He awoke to the feel of something warm and furry on his face. Instinctively, he slapped it away, then realized it was the squirrel thing. His slap had knocked it against one of the crevice walls but hadn't hurt it. It hadn't scared it either—it was bounding back toward Anand. Was it planning to bite him? Anand looked around for something to hit it with, but it stopped a foot or so away and chittered desperately, as though trying to communicate with him. It pointed its nose at the darkness outside. There was something out there it was trying to tell him about. Anand squinted, trying to see past the flames. They were still burning brightly, so he must have slept for only a little while. He could see only the tall, hulking black shapes of peaks against the cloudy night sky.

Then one of the shapes detached itself from the mountainside and began to move toward him. Another joined it, and another. They moved soundlessly but very fast. Anand had barely shaken Nisha awake before they had blocked off the exit from the crevice. In the light from the fire, he saw that they were apes—but apes unlike any he had ever seen. Their skin, though hairy like that of a gorilla, was pure white, blending in with the snow to provide a perfect camouflage. Before he could observe more, one of them came toward him, effortlessly stamping out the fire. His companion reached for Nisha.

Anand struggled, punching and kicking, but it was no use. The ape grabbed him. Was it going to eat him? Anand wondered. As far as he knew, apes weren't carnivorous, but in the strange world he had entered, reality and nightmare blended together in unexpected ways.

But the ape didn't take a bite out of him. Instead, it threw him over its shoulder and, with a growl that seemed to be a kind of command for its followers, started on its way. The other ape must have hoisted Nisha up in the same manner, because Anand could hear her yelling.

"Let me down, you overgrown, pea-brained monkey! May fleas chew your hair till you're bald all over."

Just then a red-gold shape flashed out from the darkness. The squirrel creature! It leaped at the ape that had caught Nisha. Anand craned his neck as far as possible, but he couldn't see what was going on. There was an angry grunt from the ape. It must have swiped at the squirrel, because Anand saw a red-gold blur go flying past him.

"Monster! Don't hurt my Rajah!" he heard Nisha yell, and then she was sobbing.

The apes paid no attention. They moved purposefully toward a line of hills a little distance away. Anand's ape led the pack, half shuffling and half running, jostling Anand painfully with every step. He racked his brains, trying to think of a way to escape. But it was useless. The ape gripped him firmly by his legs. And even if he could have wriggled away somehow, he couldn't abandon Nisha.

Soon they were at the hills. As the ape turned to signal to the others, Anand saw that the sheer rock face in front of him was pitted with holes. Were they cave openings? Did these strange apes live in caves, instead of among trees? His captor began to climb up the rock face, effortlessly finding footholds, while Anand dangled precariously from his back, dizzily watching the ground recede. Finally, when they were almost at the top of the rock, the ape entered one of the larger holes.

Anand expected the inside of the cave to be pitch-black, but it wasn't. There was a dim light that illuminated walls covered with primitive etchings. Before he had time to wonder where he had arrived, his captor said something in a guttural voice and dropped Anand unceremoniously onto the floor. The floor was stony, and it hurt, but Anand was too preoccupied to pay attention. What the ape said sounded almost like human speech. But apes couldn't speak, could they?

Now that he was on the floor, Anand could see that the light came from a small, smoky fire lit in an alcove. Near it was a rough-hewn rock seat, and on it sat another ape, larger by far than the ape that had captured Anand. It wore something glittery around its head that looked suspiciously like a crown. Anand guessed that this must be the king of the ape creatures.

But why had its followers brought Anand and Nisha to it?

The ape king grunted something in return. As the apes conversed, Anand was surprised to discover that if he listened carefully, he could understand a portion of what was being said, for some of the words were in the local language. He guessed that the ape king was praising its followers for catching the prisoners. Now it loped across the room to where Anand and Nisha lay. It walked almost upright, like a human, and not bent forward like the apes Anand had seen on a long-ago visit to the zoo. (But where? He realized with faint dismay that he could no longer remember the name of the city he had lived in.)

Anand couldn't help shuddering as the ape crouched over him. The ape grinned, showing sharp, glittery teeth, growling in that half-human language. "Is frightened, man-thing? No need, Grishan no hurt you. Grishan only want treasure."

Anand stared at the ape. Did it mean the conch? But that was impossible! How would an ape—even one as weird as Grishan—know of such things? "I have nothing that you'd want," he said, turning his pants pockets inside out as though to prove his point.

The ape gibbered angrily. Anand couldn't catch most of the words, but then he heard it say, "Man-thing lie! Master say you have. Master always right!"

A horrifying suspicion began to take shape in Anand's head.

"Master say, find treasure. Then Master give Grishan and his tribe weapons. Teach them more man-things. Grishan control all animals, become big king."

Were these apes Surabhanu's creatures, corrupted by his promises, twisting away from their animal nature to become caricatures of humans? Anand wondered wildly what he might tell them to persuade them to let him go, but he couldn't think of anything. Grishan's paws were searching him. His rough, callused fingers tore off a couple of coat buttons. One of the other apes was searching Nisha. She tried to fight it but stopped after an unceremonious slap from its huge paw knocked her head backward.

Now Grishan was pulling Anand's shirt out of his pants. Any moment he would see the pouch! Anand tried to breathe calmly, but he was sure the ape would hear the terrified beating of his heart and guess he was close to the "treasure."

Stop him, he called frantically to the conch. *Please, stop him from taking you away from me.*

A quiet voice said, "Oh, you humans with short memories! Did Abhaydatta not tell you that I cannot be lost against my will, nor found if I do not choose it?"

Anand felt a little better. Indeed, Grishan's hands had passed right over the pouch without pausing. Now he was searching Anand's shoes.

But the conch's comment had raised a hundred new questions in Anand's head.

But what about Surabhanu, then? How is it that he can sense you?

"Ah . . ." the conch's voice was sad. "Those initiated into the Brotherhood are linked to me, and remnants of that bond remain even if they turn to evil. But even Surabhanu cannot find me on his own now. That is why he searches for the Conch Bearer—so that you may lead him to me."

And if he finds you through me? What then? Anand asked anxiously. *Will you allow him to take you again?*

But to that the conch made no reply.

"Where you hide it?" Grishan hissed furiously. "Show, or Grishan tear you to pieces!"

Anand felt the calm weight of the conch against his belly. It gave him courage. "Tearing me to pieces will do no good. I have nothing that is of any use to you, I told you that already. Why don't you let us go?"

Grishan shook his head, glaring at Anand with beady eyes. "Man-thing tricky, Master warn Grishan. Grishan keep you till Master come. Then Master tear you himself."

He gnashed his teeth with malicious glee and gestured to the other apes. They brought thick vines and tied Anand and Nisha's hands behind their backs. For good measure, they tied their feet tightly as well. Then, leaving two apes to guard the prisoners, Grishan went off somewhere. Soon, Anand could hear drumbeats, a set of booming sounds repeated over and over. The apes were sending a message to Surabhanu. The ape guards pointed at him and jeered. He could make out a few words: *Master here soon . . . Master kill.* They passed a jar holding some kind of liquid back and forth—celebrating, Anand supposed. Their laughter and grunts grew more raucous, then fell away. But Anand hardly noticed. He slumped against the cave floor in despair. There was no way for them to escape Surabhanu now.

ᏨᎱᎪ

When Anand awoke, the fire had burned down almost to embers. He felt something moving over his chest—something furry, with small, sharp claws that dug into his skin. What new torture had Grishan devised? He started to cry out, but a hand clamped itself over his mouth. "Shhh," said a voice against his ear. "We mustn't wake the guards." It was Nisha's voice, and her hand.

How did she get free?

The furry thing was behind him now. He could feel a tug at the bonds of his hand. Something was chewing through them. In a minute, the bonds fell away. He flexed his fingers cautiously. Yes, he was free, too.

"It's Rajah!" Nisha whispered in his ear. "He found us! Can you imagine? He tracked us all the way, even though he was hurt, and saved our lives."

"Thank you," said Anand, and held out his hand to the squirrel—if that's what the animal was—who had by now chewed through the bonds around Anand's feet. Its beautiful fur was matted in places with dried blood. It must have been in pain, but it gave no sign of that. Instead, it put its forepaws on Anand's hand and looked at him gravely with its dark eyes. Anand felt, once again, that it was trying to communicate something. But there was no time to ruminate on that now. He looked for the guards and saw two hulking shapes stretched out on the ground—passed out from drinking whatever had been in the jar, he supposed. They must have thought their prisoners were safe enough. But as he watched, one of them moaned and turned on its side. The drink was wearing off.

"Hurry!" Nisha hissed. Silently, the three of them began to climb down the rock face. The squirrel ran down it effortlessly. Nisha, who was small and nimble, did well, too. Anand had the greatest difficulty. Never fond of heights, he kept his eyes on the handholds and was careful not to look down into the dizzying distance yawning below him. His legs trembled with effort and his arms ached as he scrabbled to find a hand- or foothold, and a couple of times he almost slipped. But finally he reached bottom and collapsed in a heap on the ground with a big sigh.

"No time to rest," Nisha said, tugging on his arm. "Any moment now the apes will realize we're gone and come after us."

"But which way should we go?" Anand asked, dragging himself reluctantly to his feet. "There's no point going back to the river, we'll be trapped there again. Maybe if we went back to Ranipur—"

"Look, I think Rajah's trying to tell us something," Nisha said.

Indeed, the squirrel was dashing ahead on the path and then running back to the children.

"It wants us to follow it, I think," Anand said. "But that's the way back to the river."

"I trust Rajah!" Nisha declared. "He saved us from those horrid apes, didn't he? Just as I said before, he's no ordinary animal. If he wants us to go back to the river, I'm going!" She faced Anand belligerently. "Unless you have a better idea?"

Anand had to admit that he didn't. He followed Nisha and Rajah, but with some anxiety. He tried to ask the conch what it thought of this development, but—perhaps because they now had help from elsewhere—the conch was exasperatingly silent.

"Now what do we do?" Anand asked as they stood at the riverbank, at the same spot where he and Nisha had almost drowned yesterday. The river looked no easier to cross than before. In fact, glittering in the early morning light, the swollen current was louder and faster, throwing up more spray. "Why don't you ask your precious Rajah?" he added sarcastically.

"I will!" Nisha said, and she knelt down and began to whisper to the squirrel, stroking its back. The squirrel listened intently. When she had finished, it led them a little way down the riverbank and dipped a paw into the water.

"Rajah wants us to cross here," Nisha said.

"Your Rajah's crazy," Anand said angrily. "Can't you see the river's even wider here? Can't you see the rapids? Look at those rocks in the middle—they'll tear us to pieces. If we get that far, that is."

Behind them, there was a hullabaloo, punctuated by grunts and roars. The apes had discovered their flight and were in pursuit. Soon they'd be on them.

The squirrel stepped into the water. Anand leaned forward to snatch it back—the creature had saved their life after all, and he didn't want it to be washed away to its death. But Nisha drew in her breath and grabbed his arm.

Where the squirrel had stepped, the water grew still. The squirrel began to swim across.

"Quick, after him!" Nisha said, and she stepped in, too. An amazed—and chastened—Anand followed her. The water was freezing, like yesterday, but it barely reached his calves. And the floor he stepped on was smooth and sandy, as though he was at a seashore.

Halfway across the river, Anand looked back. The apes had reached the bank. One of them waded in after the children, but he disappeared under a sudden, fierce rush of water. Anand thought he saw something long and white glistening in the current. The guardian had taken him!

The other apes screamed and threw stones but didn't dare to venture into the water. Soon, their shouts grew faint. Rajah maneuvered the children around the rocks, and in a little while they were on the other bank. Anand risked another backward glance. The current raged behind them just as it had yesterday. The apes had gone. Probably to inform "Master" of the latest developments. But even that thought did not upset Anand too much. The sun was shining, and they had crossed the first obstacle! He would worry about the next problem when it arrived.

THE SECOND OBSTACLE

Anand and Nisha rested for a while on the far bank of the river. The sun had melted the ice from the path that led away from the river—the path, Anand guessed, that they were to follow. But snow was still piled high on the rocks that bordered it. There was nothing to eat—they had lost their bags—and what was worse, Abhaydatta's—when the apes had captured them, and they were very hungry. Anand thought longingly of the stunted apple trees they'd passed earlier. Even a shriveled apple would have tasted good to him right now! Following Nisha's example, he sucked on an icicle that he broke off from an overhang of rock nearby, but that did not ease the pangs in his stomach. He wondered how long the two of them could last in this snowy wilderness without food or blankets.

"Oh, Rajah!" Nisha said with regret, stroking the squirrel's head. "You must be hungry, too. I wish I had something to give you. You've done so much for us."

Anand put out his hand, too, and touched the squirrel. "That's right," he said, though he felt strange speaking to an animal as though it were human. "We'd never have made it across the river if it weren't for you."

Rajah watched them for a minute, his head cocked to one side. Then he went off—to forage for food, Anand guessed. He stared after the scampering form, mulling over his confused thoughts. How had the squirrel managed to ford the charmed river, when he, the Conch Bearer, had failed?

"Abhaydatta said that only Beings of Power could pass the obstacle," he said softly, thinking aloud.

"*Now* what are you muttering to yourself?" Nisha said, giving him a friendly push.

"I was thinking about the squirrel."

"My Rajah? Isn't he smart! You know, I don't think he's really a squirrel."

Anand sat up and stared at her. "What do you mean?"

"Well. . . " Nisha hesitated. Then she said, "I've seen squirrels in Kolkata—there was a tree behind the soft-drink stall where some lived, and Rajah's much bigger. And his tail is different, too."

But Anand felt that she had been about to say something quite different.

Rajah was back, carrying something in his mouth. He dropped it near Nisha.

"Why, it's a nut of some kind!" she exclaimed. She hit it with a rock to crack it open and took a cautious bite of the meat inside. "Not bad!" she said to Anand, passing him a piece. "Rajah, you clever boy!"

Rajah ran ahead a little distance and waited, as though for them to follow him. They did so, and in a few minutes, they came upon a hole he had dug near a dead tree trunk. There were more nuts in the hole. The children ate them all. It wasn't as good as a full meal, Anand thought, but at least that nauseating empty feeling inside him was gone.

"We've got to move fast," he said to Nisha. "I'm sure Surabhanu will be after us soon. I don't think the river will stop him. As one of the Brotherhood, he will know how to cross it."

"But which way will we go?" Nisha said.

Anand saw that around the bend of the tree, the trail divided in two. He tried to remember the map. Surely there hadn't been two trails in it? Was his memory failing him, or was the land itself shifting? Was this part of the second obstacle? He looked around for other landmarks, but there was only a sterile expanse of snow, punctuated by boulders.

"I think we should take the left fork," he said. "It's wider."

Nisha looked doubtful, but then she nodded her head. Rajah watched them carefully. When they started on the path, he chittered in distress. He ran a little way up the other trail, then waited, his huge black eyes fixed on them.

"He wants us to go that way," Nisha whispered.

"But how can he know?" Anand objected, annoyed that she had more faith in a squirrel than in him.

"I think—" Nisha paused, then plunged on. "I think he's not a real squirrel. I think he's . . . Dadaji."

"What?" Anand's voice was incredulous.

"I think something happened to him when Surabhanu took him away. Maybe Surabhanu put a curse on him and changed him into an animal."

Anand stared at the squirrel's unblinking eyes. He wanted to scoff at Nisha's fanciful ideas as nonsense. A part of him was unsure, though. The squirrel *had* helped them cross the river. Didn't that prove he was no ordinary animal?

"But that still doesn't make him Abhaydatta," he said finally.

The squirrel's nose quivered, but it made no move.

"In any case, I think we should follow him," Nisha said.

And so they did. All through the day the squirrel led them across the snowy terrain. Sometimes they followed a trail, but often they trudged through snow that was knee-deep. The sky was a brilliant blue that hurt their eyes, and the merciless glitter of sunlight on the snow dizzied them. But they were thankful for the good weather.

"I wonder where—and what—the second obstacle is," Nisha said. "I wish we would find it soon."

Anand knew that, like him, she was wondering how they would last through the freezing night.

The squirrel led them toward a line of tall mountains to the north. Though they traveled as fast as they could through the slush that clung to their tired legs, the range did not seem to get any closer.

In the late afternoon, they turned a corner and came upon a narrow pass between two cliffs. There the squirrel stopped and chattered anxiously.

"What's the matter?" Nisha asked. "Why aren't we going through the pass? Let's take a look." She stepped forward. At once, there was a loud rumble above them. Looking up, Anand saw several boulders dislodge themselves from the top of the cliffs and fall, in a breathtaking rush of dust and gravel. He barely had time to yank Nisha out of the way before they crashed down exactly where she had been standing.

Nisha stared at them, pale-faced and trembling. "I could have been crushed to death," she whispered.

Anand was shaken, too. But he only said, "I think your wish has just come true. We've reached the second obstacle."

༄

The children tried, several times, to dash through the pass, but it was no use. Each time the mountain would come to life with a roar and rain boulders on them. They tried to find a way around the pass, but there were sheer cliff faces on both sides.

Finally, exhausted, they sank down on the snow. "I can't think of anything else," Nisha cried. Then she looked around. "Where's Rajah?"

Anand realized that he hadn't seen the squirrel in a while. A terrible thought came to him and his heart beat fast. What if the squirrel was not Abhaydatta but some other evil being, one of Surabhanu's creatures? What if it had brought them here so that it could trap them at the pass, where, cold and starving, they would be unable to resist the sorcerer?

"Rajah! Rajah!" Nisha called, and then, tentatively, "Dadaji!"

"Dadaji!" the mountains echoed back mockingly as she walked around a snowy boulder to check.

But then she called excitedly, "Anand! Come here! Take a look!"

Anand didn't answer. They were done for, he could tell. They wouldn't be able to last the night here. Already, with the sun beginning to sink, the chill in the air was increasing. Curiously, he wasn't afraid. The snow was soft and inviting, the color of gardenias, a flower his mother had loved. All he wanted to do was curl up in it and go to sleep. It didn't matter if he didn't wake up.

But Nisha was pulling at his arm. "You mustn't sleep! You mustn't!" she cried. "Come and see what Rajah's found."

Anand pulled away. He was too tired. Nothing in the world mattered to him more than sleep. Then he felt something against his stomach, like a small electric shock. The conch! In his hopelessness, he had forgotten it. Now it sent a buzzing warmth through his limbs, stirring his frozen heart.

"I can't give up, not while I'm still responsible for you," he whispered. Then he followed Nisha.

There were several low boulders strewn to one side, all thickly covered in snow. The squirrel had been scrabbling at them with his paws, trying to uncover them. But his feet were too little, and he hadn't gotten far.

The children had no idea what he was looking for, but they joined him, scraping away snow with fingers that soon turned numb. Each time they uncovered a boulder, Rajah would examine it carefully, then move away and scrabble at another one.

Anand could no longer feel his fingers. He could see that his nails were raw and torn, though it was too cold for his fingers to bleed. "This is useless!" he said to Nisha, scraping dispiritedly. "I can't do any more. I don't even know what we're trying to find!"

Nisha didn't answer. She was looking at the boulder they had just uncovered. To one side of the boulder was a small mark. The squirrel was throwing himself against the mark, making excited sounds.

"It looks like a handprint, doesn't it?" Nisha said. "Maybe he wants us to touch it."

Anand placed his palm against the print and looked around.

"Nothing's happening," he said disappointedly.

"Your hand's too big," Nisha said. "See how your fingers reach beyond the mark? Let me try." She put her hand on the print. It fit perfectly, and she looked around to see if anything was different. Finally she shook her head and pulled her hand away.

"I guess I was wrong," she said.

"Stop!" Anand said, staring at the ground. "Put your hand back. I think I see something."

As Nisha touched the mark again, he saw a thin, pale line begin to glow along the ground. It started at the boulder and continued past the corner. When Anand followed it, he saw that it led into the pass.

"Nisha!" he exclaimed excitedly. "I think you've just found us a way to overcome the second obstacle!"

"What do you mean?"

"See the line? I think if we step only on it and nowhere else, we'll be safe."

"What line?" Nisha said, staring blankly at Anand.

She couldn't see it! The line was visible only to Anand!

"It's all right," he said. "Just follow me, and put your foot exactly where I place mine."

He began walking. But as soon as Nisha lifted her hand from the boulder to follow him, the line faded away.

Anand stared at the empty path. How were they going to manage this?

"What's the matter?" Nisha asked. "Why did you stop?"

"I can see the line only as long as you keep touching the handprint," he said, shaking his head in frustration.

The children stood there for a while, stumped. Then, slowly, a solution dawned on Anand, but he couldn't bring himself to say it. Nisha, however, had thought of the same thing.

"I'll keep touching the boulder. You and Rajah go through the pass," she said.

"But what about you?"

She shrugged. "Getting that shell—or whatever it is that you're carrying—back to the Silver Valley is more important."

"I can't leave you," Anand protested. With a sinking feeling in his stomach, he remembered that he had once said the same thing to Abhaydatta.

"I'll be fine for a little while." Nisha pressed her lips together to keep them from quivering and spoke as bravely as she could. "Once you get to the valley, you can come back with help."

Looking at her, Anand felt ashamed of all the times he had thought ill of her, or wished she were not with him. And now here she was, willing to sacrifice herself for him. He glanced around desperately. Surely there was some other way! What if he could mark the path? But there was nothing around him but snow and boulders that were too large to move.

"Listen carefully," he finally said. "I'll take a handful

of the snow we've scraped from the boulders, and wherever I step, I'll place a little pile of it. As soon as I've gone through the pass, you follow, and be really careful to step only on the piles."

"I will!" Nisha said, brightening. "Anand, it's really smart of you to think of that!"

Anand grinned. "Why, I do believe that's the first compliment you've ever paid me!"

Anand scooped up as much snow as his hands could hold and hurried along the path. His fingers turned numb almost immediately, and it was hard to get them to do what he wanted. Instead of making neat little piles, he ended up dropping big globs of snow behind him. What was worse, he ran out of snow before he reached the end of the pass. Desperately, he tried to scrape up more, but there was only ice in the pass, rock hard and impossible for him to dislodge. His nails broke on the ice; skin tore from his fingertips. Perhaps I can mark the path with blood, he thought wildly. But it was so cold that his fingers wouldn't even bleed. The glowing line ahead of him began to dim as he scrabbled around. Finally, afraid that he would be trapped in the pass, Anand gave up and went on.

Once he had made it through the pass, he called out to Nisha to follow quickly. The line had faded even before she took the first step into the pass. She placed her feet carefully on the piles of snow Anand had made, moving confidently until she came to the spot where he had run out of snow. She looked at him, frowning in confusion.

"I'm sorry," he called. "There wasn't any more snow. You'll have to make a run for it—it's only a small distance. Move as fast as you can."

Nisha nodded, and leaning forward, sprinted as quickly as she could. But the mountain was faster. She had scarcely moved her foot when boulders began to fall, so fast and hard that it seemed like the entire mountainside was sliding down. Nisha covered her head with her arms and dashed forward. A rock hit her shoulder and threw her off-course, but she recovered and kept moving. She was going to make it! Anand thought jubilantly.

Then he saw the black boulder. It moved rapidly, but unlike the others it didn't just fall downward. It moved diagonally across the cliff face toward Nisha, defying gravity, as though it could sense her. As though it had intelligence. And just as she sprinted to reach the end of the pass where Anand was waiting anxiously, it hurled itself directly at her leg. There was a sickening crack, and Nisha fell over with a scream of pain, her leg twisting unnaturally under her.

Desperately, Anand reached into the pass and dragged her out. He wasn't a moment too early, for an entire chunk of cliff side broke off with a roar and came hurtling down. There was a deafening crash, then silence. Through the cloud of gravelly snow, Anand could see that the pass was completely blocked off. There was no way for them to retreat now. He wondered for a moment if the blockage would keep Surabhanu at bay.

He knelt in front of Nisha, who was sobbing with pain.

"Can you stand up if I take your weight?" he asked her. She shook her head, and when he touched her foot lightly, she screamed. "It hurts terribly, terribly," she said. "I think it's broken. I'm sorry. You'll just have to go the last bit on your own." Then her eyes widened. She was shivering so hard with the cold and the shock that she couldn't raise her hand, but he could tell she was trying to point at something behind him.

Anand turned to look. On this side of the pass, it seemed even colder than before—if that were possible. His breath made a cloud of vapor, and when he drew in the thin, cold air, it pricked his lungs like icy needles. Directly ahead of him was the three-pronged peak that Abhaydatta had drawn for them—so long ago that it seemed to be another life. In the clear air, it seemed to him that he could reach out his hand and touch it. He was almost at the end of his journey! He stared at the three beautiful peaks shining like a crown of burnished silver in the sun, and tears came to his eyes.

THE SCARLET SNAKE

Anand took off his coat and wrapped it around Nisha.

"I'll come back as soon as I can," he said, his teeth chattering in the icy wind. "It shouldn't take long. Abhaydatta said that all I have to do is reach the bottom of the first peak and call out for the Healers. They'll be waiting for us. Meanwhile, your Rajah will keep you company." As he spoke, he looked around for the animal, but he didn't see it anywhere. Where could it have gone? He thought he'd seen it scamper through the pass ahead of him, but he'd been preoccupied and so wasn't sure. Oh no! Was it trapped on the other side of the magic pass?

Nisha didn't respond. Her mouth was slack, and there was a glazed look in her half-closed eyes. She shivered all over, like a patient with malarial fever, but when he touched her hand fearfully, it was cold and rubbery, as though it did not belong to a human being.

Anand was torn in two. She was obviously unwell. Perhaps it was the shock from the broken leg. How could he leave her alone? And yet, if he didn't get to the peak—

and to the Healers—he would not be able to get help for her, and she might die.

"Tell me what to do," he whispered to the conch.

The conch was silent, but another voice spoke. "I'll tell you what to do—just hand over the conch to me, and I'll take care of all your problems." Startled, he looked down. The voice had come from Nisha's mouth, but it wasn't hers. It was a toneless, dead sound, and it chilled him. She was sitting up now, her eyes glittering and unfocused, her arm stretched out toward him. "Give it here," she said again, her mouth grimacing.

Anand shuddered as her fingers curled around his forearm. Her grip was very strong. Any tighter, and his bones would break.

"Nisha!" he cried in pain and amazement. "What's wrong with you?"

"Wrong!" Nisha's mouth twisted in a smile that looked horribly familiar, though he couldn't quite place it. "Nothing's wrong! In fact, finally, things are about to become right. The conch will go back to its rightful master—my master! And then . . . Ah, we'll have some fun then!"

Surabhanu! That was whom her smile reminded him of. Somehow, Surabhanu had taken over Nisha's mind. Had it happened only now, or a long time ago? There was no time to wonder. Nisha's viselike grip was pulling him to the ground while her other hand groped over his chest. Anand knew he had to get away.

"I know you have it," the voice coming out of her mouth hissed. "But for some reason I can't see it. You've hidden it somehow. Damn your wicked slyness!" Then the lips stretched out again in that nightmarish smile. "But no matter, the master is coming. He'll know what to do. I merely have to hold you here for a little while—until he takes over. That should not be too difficult."

Her other hand moved jerkily toward him and grasped his shoulder. Her fingers were like frozen iron. They sent a chill through his shirt all the way to his heart. With every last bit of his strength, he tried to get away, but the force that had taken over Nisha was too powerful for him. A haze was filling his vision. He felt as though he couldn't breathe. He looked past her face, so terrifying in its inhuman blankness, to see if there was anyone—or anything—he could call on for help. But there wasn't. He stared hopelessly at the red river that wound its sinuous way down the sheer snowy side of the cliff. But wait—there had been no river there even a few moments ago! He wondered if the lack of oxygen was making him hallucinate. The river looked too solid, though, to be a hallucination. It reached the ground and flowed toward him, rippling and curving. Then it raised up its enormous hood and he realized what it was.

Behind him, he heard the creature Nisha had turned into say, "Master, we meet again!"

The giant snake fixed Anand with its cold, glittering eyes and said, "Ah yes, we meet again, Anand. Under happier circumstances this time, though not as soon as I would have liked. You almost made it to that cursed valley, but thanks to my little servant here, you were held back!"

Anand struggled vainly, once again, to get away from Nisha's grip.

"She's strong, my servant, isn't she?" the snake laughed. "In case you were wondering, it's my power that fills her." He flicked his tongue at Nisha and she stood with a jerk, pulling Anand up with her. Anand glanced at her injured leg. It was straight and appeared to have healed.

"You see, Anand," the snake taunted. "*I* take care of my servants, not like that old idiot who abandoned you to your own devices. You, too, should have chosen to serve me! You would be better off today if you had!"

"Nisha didn't *choose* to serve you. You forced her." Anand managed to choke out the words.

"A mere technicality! I got inside her head the very first time we met, and made a comfortable little nest there, biding my time. I got inside your head, too, for a few moments—then, and again later. But each time I tried to settle in, somehow I found myself thrown out." The serpent hissed with displeasure. "But no matter. Whatever—or whoever— protected you is gone now."

Help me! Anand cried silently to the conch. *Now more than ever before, I need you!*

The conch was silent.

For your own sake, if not for mine, show your power!
Anand called angrily inside his head. *Do you want to be back
in Surabhanu's clutches again?*

"Chessmen may move only one at a time," the conch's
voice said, sounding as though it came from far away. "It
is someone else's turn now."

"Stupid boy!" the snake spat. "Talking to that thing
as though it were alive and intelligent! Being around
Abhaydatta has addled your brain. The conch is a *thing*, to
be used by the one who possesses it. I told this to those
fools at the Brotherhood, but they wouldn't listen. It's an
object of power, yes, but only an object, after all. I know
because I studied it carefully, for all those years when I was
stuck in that loathsome valley. But my reward now is that
I know exactly how to use it! As you will find out in a
moment."

Surabhanu couldn't hear the conch! The realization
gave Anand a moment of hope, though he hadn't quite
understood what the conch meant by its talk of chessmen.
But his hope faded as the snake slithered closer to him.
It was almost upon him now. "When I touch you," it said,
"I will know where you've hidden the conch, and when I
touch the conch, it will become mine. Then I'll be able to
regain my own shape and not be limited by this form
to which I've been confined ever since my battle with
Abhaydatta!"

Anand struggled desperately, but he couldn't escape Nisha's stone-hard grasp. *It's over!* he thought. In a moment the snake's slimy mouth would be on him.

Then a flash of furry gold flew through the air like an arrow, launching itself at the snake's head. It was the squirrel! It fought the snake expertly, hissing and spitting, forcing it to back away from an amazed Anand.

"Rajah!" he breathed. "You came back! Thank you!" Then, as he stared at the feisty little animal, something he'd read a long time ago in a book came back to him. "Why, you're not a squirrel!" he whispered. "You're a mongoose!"

The snake called to Nisha. "Quick! Help me! Pick up the boulder near your foot and hit the boy on the head with it. Hit him hard and knock him out. I'll deal with him once I take care of this creature."

He pulled back his head to strike at the mongoose. Anand could see his gleaming fangs, their tips blue with poison. But the mongoose darted in fearlessly and sank its teeth into the snake's neck. Black blood spurted out. The snake gave a roar of pain and began to throw its body from side to side, trying to dislodge the mongoose. Its tail lashed, whiplike, at the animal. The mongoose held on, its small, sharp teeth buried in the snake's flesh, for as long as it could. But it was no match for the giant snake. Anand could see it beginning to slip.

Beside him, Nisha had bent over and, with one hand,

picked up a huge boulder twice the size of her head. Her other hand still gripped Anand's arm. She hefted the boulder effortlessly, fueled by Surabhanu's power. Any moment now she'd bring it down on Anand's skull. He tried to wrest his arm from her grasp once more, but he knew it was useless.

"Nisha," he pleaded. "Don't do this, please! Surabhanu's evil. Can't you see that? Look, even Rajah can sense it. He's trying to protect us from him!"

With one immense, final shake of its head, the snake had thrown off the mongoose. It flew through the air, smashed into the side of the cliff, and fell to the ground. As it struggled, dazed, to get to its feet, the snake struck. Its fangs sank into the mongoose's shoulder. The mongoose gave a small cry and fell with a shudder.

Next to Anand, Nisha's body shuddered, too.

The snake raised its bleeding head and spoke contemptuously. "A fitting end to you, Abhaydatta, old fool! Once again you chose to tangle with me when you could have scampered off to your precious valley and saved your skin. But this is better! This way I've gained a double pleasure—your death and the ownership of the conch!"

Abhaydatta! Anand stared at the limp mongoose in horror and love. Nisha's hunch had been right, after all. The old man must have taken on an animal form to battle the evil sorcerer, and then, like Surabhanu, been trapped in that shape by his weakness! Grief broke over him like a wave, but he pushed it back. *Not now! Now I must try to save the conch*, he said in his mind to the Master Healer. *It is what you would have wanted.*

The snake spoke to Nisha commandingly. "Girl! Why are you standing there like a half-wit, with your mouth open? Hit him with the rock!"

"You killed him!" Nisha said softly. "You killed my beautiful Rajah!" Glancing at her, Anand saw that tears were running down her cheeks.

"I can explain it all," the snake said smoothly, swaying its head in a mesmerizing rhythm. "As soon as you knock the boy unconscious." Though it still bled from the mongoose's bites, it was slowly moving forward again.

"Nisha!" Anand cried. "Don't look in its eyes!"

Nisha didn't respond. She hefted the boulder in both her hands, letting go of Anand for better aim. Anand didn't wait another moment. He ran as fast as he could— but he didn't get far before he slipped on the ice and fell. He curled up on the ground trying to protect his head with his arms. Over his shoulder, he could hear a hissing as the snake dragged its injured body toward him.

He heard a scream, then a thud, then a longer yell, drawn out in its fury. He stiffened, waiting for the pain to course through him, then realized that the rock had not hit him. He raised his head to see what was happening.

Nisha was standing where he'd left her, with a look of mingled horror and triumph on her face. She was watching the snake, which writhed on the ground, hissing terribly. The boulder had landed on its tail.

"I'll get you for this!" the snake screamed, trying to pull its tail out from under the boulder. "You'll soon feel the weight of Surabhanu's wrath!"

"I don't care!" Nisha said. Her voice shook a little with fear, but she raised her chin resolutely. "That was for what you did to my Rajah." Then she turned to Anand. "Run!" she shouted.

Anand ran, keeping his knees bent, careful to stay low so that he wouldn't slip again. Behind him he heard crashing sounds, then a cry. He steeled himself and did not look back. They'd done so much for him and for the conch, Nisha and Rajah both. If he didn't reach the peak in time, their sacrifices would be in vain.

He was almost at the foot of the peak when he felt a paralyzing shaft of pain shoot through him. It was the same kind of pain he'd felt in the train compartment with Surabhanu. It brought him to his knees. Then, though he didn't want to look back, he felt his head turning—as though he were a doll and some giant child were playing with him.

Nisha was stretched out on the snow, not far from Rajah's body. And the snake—but no, it wasn't a snake anymore. Instead, it was a gaseous cloud that loomed over Anand. As he watched, the cloud grew more solid, taking human shape. The face was still indistinct, but he could see the glitter of Surabhanu's diadem already, atop the head.

A voice boomed all around him. "Now that Abhaydatta is gone, I have more power! Enough power to rid myself of that limiting snake shape, though I guess it was useful enough in its way." The voice cackled with laughter. "With every passing moment, I can feel myself growing stronger. There's no point in trying to escape me, Anand. Give me the conch!"

Against his will, Anand's hand moved toward the pouch. *No!* he cried to himself. *Stop! He can't take it from you unless you give it to him.* He focused on his hand with his whole mind, and to his surprise and relief, felt it stop moving.

"You've learned some new tricks, haven't you, boy!" the specter jeered, but Anand could tell it was taken aback by his small victory. He knew he'd have to move fast, while Surabhanu was figuring out what to do next. He concentrated on the conch, drawing comfort from the memory of their conversations, the love he had felt for it and continued to feel even now, even though it had not helped him in his need. He tried to move his arms and legs and found that, although it was painful, he was able to crawl forward slowly. He focused his blurring vision on the flat stone at the base of the cliff, the one Abhaydatta had told him about. It was very close now.

"Stop!" screamed the specter, its voice echoing from the mountaintops. It, too, had gathered its resources. "Look at me, Anand, I command you!"

Anand tried to focus his mind again, to shut out Surabhanu's words, to make his body continue crawling, but it was impossible to concentrate. It was as though a giant fist were hammering away inside his head.

"If you give it to me right now," the voice said, "I'll be kind and kill you quickly. If not. . . ." It paused and the hot space inside Anand's head was filled with horrifying images of his mangled body and screaming face.

The specter was thicker now, almost a physical body. It hovered lower, and the cloud arms reached down toward Anand. He could feel a weight radiating from them, smashing him into the frozen earth with such force that he couldn't breathe. He wouldn't be able to reach the stone step, after all.

I did everything I could, he said sadly to the conch with his last thought. *And still I failed you.*

Was it because he wanted it so much that he heard the voice speaking back to him? The cool, seashore voice of the conch. Could such a voice, made from the elements themselves, care about anything that happened in this mortal world?

"You didn't fail. But yes, you did everything you could. And so I am now permitted to do something for you."

Anand thought he felt the pressure on him lessen just a little. He drew in an aching chestful of breath. Was the conch really speaking?

"Stand up, Anand," the conch said, "and take me

out. Don't be afraid. Use me. I give you permission."

"How shall I use you?" Anand asked. But already, an image had flashed inside his head.

As though in a dream, he rose slowly and took the conch from the pouch. It glowed eerily white in the shadow of the cloud. Did it pulse faintly in the frozen air? He put it to his mouth and blew.

An enormous roar came from the conch, a blast of sound so forceful that Anand thought its reverberation would crack every bone in his body. He could see the air ripple as it moved toward Surabhanu's shadow-form. Sparks filled the space through which it moved. When the fiery ripple reached the dark, hovering specter of Surabhanu, there was a huge flash. The surge from the explosion struck Anand, knocking him off his feet. *I'm dying*, he thought, gasping with pain as he hit the ground. He felt the conch falling from his hand, and everything turned dark.

THE FINAL TEST

When Anand came to, Nisha was kneeling by him in the pale silver light of a moon about to set, patting his face. He tried to jerk upright, but she pushed him back, and he was too weak to resist.

"Rest a moment," she said. "Or you might get dizzy and faint again."

He managed to force his stiff, disobedient lips to form a question. "Where's the conch?"

"Right here, on your chest," Nisha said. She guided his hand until it closed around the conch.

"Did you put it there?"

Nisha shook her head. "You must have clutched it to you as you fell."

But Anand knew better. The conch chooses to be lost or to be found, to stay or to go, he thought. He picked it up carefully and looked at it, his heart beating with joy. His vision was still blurry, but he could tell that the conch looked small and ordinary again. He fumbled with his pouch—why, he was as uncoordinated as a baby—and finally managed to slip the conch inside.

Thank you for choosing to stay with me, he said in his mind.

"You're welcome," the conch said. "Not that I had a plethora of choices. Slimy Red was never a contender, so it had to be you or Miss Mule Head—and I distinctly remember her calling me a shell. A *shell*, if you please!"

Anand could feel his dry lips crack as a smile broke across his face.

"Look!" Nisha was pulling at his hand.

There was a large fissure beside him, empty of snow and burned black.

"Did you see what happened?" he asked.

She hesitated. "I'm not sure. I thought I saw a great fire, or perhaps it was lightning, come from your mouth. The snake creature burst into flame—but there was too much smoke, I couldn't really tell. It howled and took off for the sky, or maybe it was sucked down into the earth."

They stared at the fissure. Was Surabhanu really destroyed? Anand couldn't quite believe it.

As though she sensed his thoughts, Nisha said, "I think he's gone for good, but you'd better not waste any time." She started to cough and couldn't stop. Anand could see that her face had grown pale, and in spite of the cold there were beads of sweat on her upper lip. When she spoke again, her words came in gasps, as though she had run out of breath. "You'd better get the conch to the foot of the peak."

Reluctantly, Anand pushed himself up onto his knees. His arms and legs felt too weak to bear his weight, and he ached all over, as though he'd been thrown against the side of the mountain. He knew there was something else he should be asking Nisha, but his head was so heavy he couldn't remember it.

When he held out his arm to pull her up, she shook her head.

"Aren't you coming with me?" he asked, surprised.

Nisha shook her head with a grimace.

"My leg—I can't move it too well. It hurts a lot even when I'm sitting, but if I try to put any weight on it, it's just terrible. I could barely drag myself over to you."

She pulled the edge of her dress back from her knee. Even in the half dark, Anand could see the unnatural angle at which her leg was bent. Dismayed, he cried, "But wasn't it healed?"

"I think that was temporary, and it went away when Surabhanu left. Or maybe it was never healed. Maybe it was all an illusion, a trick of his to get me to do what he wanted. In any case, I'd rather have both legs broken than be in his power." She gave a shudder. "I'm awfully sorry for what I did to you."

"I know you couldn't help it," Anand interrupted. "I know how that is. Horrible, isn't it, when you have no control over your arms and legs—even your words? But—"

Nisha swayed and gave a small moan. "Awfully sorry, I

think I've got to lie down. Can you take . . . him . . . with you?" She pointed to the small golden-brown mass of fur that lay unmoving at the foot of the cliff. "I tried to wake him," she said tiredly, "but I couldn't. Maybe the Healers can help him."

Abhaydatta! How could he have forgotten him even for a moment! Anand ran to the mongoose and picked him up. The small, limp body weighed almost nothing. For a moment, with a sinking of his heart, he thought there was no life left in the creature. Then he saw its chest rise and fall in the faintest of movements.

Anand couldn't stop his tears. He wasn't completely sure yet that the mongoose was, indeed, the Master Healer—it seemed so *impossible*. And yet, hadn't almost everything that happened to him in the last few weeks been impossible, too?

As he stared at the mongoose, memories flooded him. How many times had the old man protected Nisha and him, had seen to their comfort even when he himself was under stress or in danger! How many times had he forgiven Anand his stupidities and doubts! Even at the very last, he had thrown himself fearlessly at the snake just to save Anand's life!

"I won't let you die," he whispered fiercely, "I won't!"

Stumbling, with the mongoose cradled in his arms, he made for the peak. Yes, there was the flat rectangular rock, shaped like a step, at its foot, just as Abhaydatta had described. With a rapidly beating heart, he stood upon it.

All through the dangers of the journey, at moments when he felt so overwhelmed that he wanted to give up, Anand had kept himself going by imagining this moment. In his mind's eye, Abhaydatta would stand on the rock, with Anand and Nisha on either side of him, and raise the conch above his head. As the light of the rising sun haloed the conch and streaked his white head with gold, he would call to his brother Healers. With a sound like thunder or cheers from a thousand throats, an opening in the shape of a giant gate would appear in the mountain's side. Plumed horses and jeweled elephants would march out in a procession to carry the Master Healer and his companions in triumph through the valley. The fantasy changed a little each time Anand daydreamed it, but in no version of it had he stood on the rock alone to announce his arrival.

But it was no use wishing for what could not be. He cleared his throat. "Open the pass, Healers. I have brought you that for which you have been waiting."

There was no reply. Had he gotten the words wrong? Perhaps there was some formula, some proper and reverential way to announce the conch's presence. He put his hand on the conch for help, but it was silent. What had it said? Only when humans had done all they could do was it allowed to use its power to help. Anand would just have to try again.

"Are you there?" he called. "Can you hear me?

Brothers of the conch—I have brought back to you that which was stolen. Open the gate and let us in."

Still there was no answer. The moon had disappeared, and in the faint glow of the stars the stretches of ice around Anand looked barren, a wasteland where nothing lived. He felt like a fool, standing in front of a wall of rock, calling to people who perhaps did not even exist. He wanted to give up and turn around.

The mongoose stirred in his arms and gave a small, shuddering moan.

No! Anand said to himself. Doubting things—that had always been his weakness. All through this journey he'd doubted the words of the Master Healer and trusted his own intelligence, the little, tinny voice of logic that said *this isn't real.* And each time it had led him into one trouble after another, had caused him to almost ruin everything. He would not doubt any longer. The animal in his arms was real; the girl with the broken leg, lying on the icy path behind him, waiting for him to succeed, was real. As real as anything in this secret, baffling landscape could be. Equally real was the fact that he was the only one left who could help them. And if that meant shouting at a mountain till he lost his voice, Anand would do it.

"My companions are hurt and in need of your help," he shouted once more. "We've risked our lives to bring you the conch, without which you, too, cannot survive. Let us into the valley, please!"

The silence stretched out for an interminable moment. Then a voice spoke from somewhere in the mountain peak. Anand strained to understand the muffled, booming words.

"Set the conch down on the step, boy, and return to where you came from."

Anand couldn't believe his ears. After all they had done, risking their lives, the ungrateful speaker wanted him to hand over the conch, turn around, and go back? As though he'd merely strolled up from a village down the road! Didn't they even care that Abhaydatta, a member of their own Brotherhood, was injured almost to death? And even if they hadn't been hurt and exhausted, didn't the Conch Bearer and his companions deserve better treatment than this? Didn't Anand, who had, after all, vanquished Surabhanu, deserve a few accolades? Anger surged in him. For a moment he was tempted to raise the conch once again to his lips, teach the insolent speaker a lesson.

"Ah, Anand, think with care! What does he want you to do?" The cool voice of the conch felt to Anand like he was sucking on an ice chip on a blazing summer's day in Kolkata. It cleared his head.

"Thank you," he said to it. "Thank you for warning me that this is another test. The voice wants to see if I get angry, if I lose control." He smiled a tight smile. "Well, it isn't going to happen."

"I am not going to leave," he called out to the invisible voice. "We have fought too hard and risked everything— our bodies and minds, even our spirits—to get here. The reason we came was not for ourselves but to help the Brotherhood, I would remind you. So, I won't give up the conch. Not until you help my companions. Not until you let us into the valley." He raised the mongoose's body up high. "Abhaydatta promised us this."

There was a pause, as though the voice had not expected this response. Then it said, "It is easy to speak of promises, boy, using the name of one who is no longer with us. But only the deserving are allowed to pass beyond this point. However, since you have come this far, we will give you a chance. We will ask you a question, and give you until daybreak for your reply. If you are able to answer correctly, you may enter the Silver Valley."

Hot words of argument rose to Anand's lips. He wanted to tell that cold, superior voice exactly how deserving he was. Hadn't Abhaydatta himself come to his home and asked him for help in his quest? Hadn't Anand dueled with the evil genius Surabhanu, who had fooled and foiled the Brotherhood, and won? Wasn't he the one the conch spoke to?

"And the one who doesn't listen when I speak," the conch said, its words cool but also hard, like stones in a riverbed that might cut an unwary traveler's feet.

Anand bit his lip. *What a fool I am! I almost fell into the trap again, didn't I?*

This time the conch's voice was like the whisper of a hummingbird's wings. "It's a wise fool who knows his own folly."

Anand drew himself up to his full height and turned to the impassive rock face. "Speak your question, and I will do my best to answer it."

"Very well," the voice said. Or was it a chorus of voices? "Which of these three virtues is the most important: honesty, loyalty, or compassion? Remember, by daybreak—which is one hour away—you must bring us your answer."

"But can you not help my companions before then?" Anand cried. "They are in pain, and Abhaydatta has been poisoned. Another hour might be too late."

"We do not know why you keep speaking the name of Abhaydatta," the voice said. "He is gone. That creature in your hands is only a mongoose, and may be beyond saving already. And the girl—she is of no importance to us. However, to ease your mind, we will wrap them in a sleep cloud while you wrestle with the question we have given you. They will not feel pain, nor will they degenerate further. But if your answer is the wrong one, you must promise to ask no more of us. You must give us the conch and leave."

The voice spoke in a tone of finality. Anand knew it

would be of no use trying to bargain further.

"I promise," he said. He glanced at the sky. Was it his imagination, or was it already growing light in the East? He turned his mind to the question, the final test that he hadn't expected.

THE GREATEST VIRTUE

Anand paced up and down on the ice, his mind in turmoil. Quite a bit of time had passed since the voice had challenged him with the question about the three virtues, and the clouds in the East were distinctly tinged with orange. Any moment now, the sun would raise his golden head above the peaks of the Himalayas. And then? What would he do then? He was no closer to an answer than when he started.

"Honesty, loyalty, compassion," he muttered to himself. "Which is the best?" He looked desperately at Nisha. Her body lay limp and unmoving on the cold, hard ground. Her face, pale and expressionless, seemed so far beyond his reach. It looked uncannily like Meera's face had in the days when she had been a prisoner inside her own head, before Abhaydatta freed her. For a moment his mind sped along the paths of memory, and he wondered how his sister fared. Did she think of him, and if so, was it with love—or blame?

But Anand knew he couldn't afford the luxury of such

musings. He had a task ahead of him, and the fate of his companions depended on his success. The voice from the mountain had said that Nisha would not get worse until daybreak. Still, Anand tucked the coat he had given her more carefully around her body. He wished he could have consulted with her. She was smart and often saw things that he was blind to. She had been a good companion to him all through the journey, brave and tenacious when he had been disheartened. *I should have told her that when I had the chance, instead of being angry and jealous and impatient,* he thought with a pang.

The mongoose was lying on the stone step, its body, too, held in the same deep unconsciousness. *If only Abhaydatta had been with him!* He would have known right away what the greatest virtue was. But then there would have been no occasion for this unfair test. They would have been welcomed into the valley with open arms. By now they would have been sitting in the feast hall, dining on steaming rice and dal; fried potatoes; hot puffy pooris; not to mention plump gulab jamuns soaked in syrup, and. . . .

Stop! Anand told his disobedient mind. *Stay focused on the problem!* Abhaydatta couldn't help him right now, but there were so many things he had taught Anand on the way. Surely he had spoken about one of these virtues? But though he racked his brains, Anand couldn't remember.

He grasped the conch in his hand. *I know you can't*

help me. This is my test, and I must pass it, he said silently. But if I fail, at least take care of the others. Make sure they aren't left out here to die.

Just as he had expected, the conch did not answer, though he thought he felt a current of sympathy flow from it into his cold hands, warming them for the moment. Which virtue would the conch have chosen? Perhaps it would have gone for honesty—it had always spoken directly and plainly to Anand. Or, not being human, would it know about human virtues at all?

"I know enough to think beyond what I am expected to think," the conch said enigmatically. But though Anand waited, hoping for more, it didn't elaborate further.

Which virtue would Nisha have chosen? Anand wondered. It was hard to guess—she was a girl of many moods. But perhaps she would have chosen loyalty. She had always stayed with him, and she had risked her life to help Anand and avenge Abhaydatta. And Abhaydatta—he was so kind to them, surely he would have chosen compassion. But no, he was loyal, too. He could have saved himself many times over, as Surabhanu had jeeringly pointed out. On the night when he came to them in mongoose form, he could have taken the conch and escaped to the Silver Valley, but he had chosen to remain with Anand and Nisha. But he had always been honest, too, never downplaying the dangers the children would face, never pretending to be all powerful.

Anand stared at the mongoose, hoping for a sign of some sort, but the animal lay still as death. More than at any time in his life, Anand realized, he was on his own, with only his wits to save himself and his dear companions.

As though in response to that thought, the golden arc of the sun appeared above the eastern peak.

From inside the mountain, the voice spoke. "It is daybreak, Anand. We await your answer. Which virtue did you choose?"

Anand felt a great weight settle on his heart. Time had run out, and he had found no answer. He took the conch out to look at it one last time, for he knew he would have to give it up. He ran a forefinger along its smoothness, admiring how the pinkness of its inner wall blended smoothly with the white of its outside. If only he could have deciphered what it meant when it said *I know enough to think beyond what I am expected to think*. He dared not look at his sleeping companions. He was afraid then that he might not be able to stop his tears. And he did not want to weep in front of the pitiless voice that waited for his answer.

Though sorrow filled him, and anxiety, Anand stood up tall and faced the peak that guarded the Silver Valley. He clutched the conch to his chest for comfort, and felt, one last time, a wave of energy flow from it, giving him strength.

"I didn't choose any of the three virtues," he replied.

"Why not?" Was the voice angry? It was hard to tell, since it was as toneless as ever. "Your task was to choose. You *must* choose!"

Anand's throat was dry with fear, but he shook his head resolutely. "I can't choose just one. The three virtues are connected—one can't exist fully without the other. Without one, the others lose their flavor. Honesty without compassion is too harsh to do any good. Compassion without loyalty lacks power, so you can't help the people you care for. Loyalty without honesty may make you follow the wrong person, or the wrong cause." He paused, but there was no response from the mountain. How could he explain his thoughts better? He looked at the conch in his hand. "It's like the colors on the conch—the way the pink and white blend to make a beautiful whole. That's how Abhaydatta was, and Nisha—" His voice broke and he couldn't say any more.

Still there was silence from within the peak.

Sadly, Anand took off his shirt and wrapped it around the mongoose. But as he replaced the conch in its pouch, a sentence flashed like electricity in his brain. *What if I don't give it up?* As though in response, he felt the conch grow heavy in his hand and cold as death. *Maybe with its help I can—* With a great, wrenching effort, he pulled his mind from that thought and made himself set the conch down on the stone step.

"Here is the conch," he said. "I'll go away, as I had promised. Please take care of my companions in whatever way you can. Remember, without them, the conch wouldn't be here now."

He turned and looked down the path toward the blocked pass. How would he get over all those boulders? Well, he would work it out when he got there, one step at a time. And if he failed? Well, one more failure wouldn't matter, would it? At least the conch was safely back where it belonged. That part would have made Abhaydatta and Nisha happy.

But what was that great, rumbling sound behind him, like an earthquake? He whirled around, and gasped at the sight that met his eyes. The peak had split open, and in the opening was a tall and beautiful doorway, shining and many-faceted as though cut from crystal. In the doorway stood three men dressed in white robes, their long white hair loose and shining in the morning sun. They were smiling.

"You have answered rightly," the one on the left said.

"Truly, without its companions to balance it, a powerful virtue can become a weakness," the one on the right added.

The man in the center, who was the tallest and oldest, raised his hands in welcome. "You are wise beyond your years, Anand. It is our pleasure to welcome you to Silver Valley."

Anand couldn't believe his ears. Was this another cruel hallucination? He rubbed his eyes, but the doorway was still there, and the men. And behind them the Silver Valley unfurled itself, as bright as a flag. Anand drew in his breath at what he saw. It was as though he were looking into a different world. The first things he noticed were the trees. Untouched by winter, they were laden with silver flowers that were unlike any blossoms he'd ever seen before. And they were everywhere, bordering the lakes and winding paths that led to the simple but elegant wooden halls where, he guessed, the Healers lived.

"Why, it's beautiful!" he said. "More beautiful even than what Abhaydatta described."

"Ah, you are looking at our parijat trees," the man on the left said, and for a moment an expression of great love transformed his face. "It is said they were brought from the heavenly garden of Indra, and of all places on Earth, it is only in our valley that they have survived. But you must not blame Abhaydatta, for truly it is difficult to describe their beauty." Then his face grew stern again. "Come quickly. The auspicious moment of sunrise will soon pass, and then we must close the gate."

Shaking with joy and excitement, Anand stepped forward. But then he paused. "What about my companions?" he asked with a frown. "Is someone going to carry them into the valley and get them to a Healer? I don't want to go in before they're taken care of."

The man on the right shook his head sadly. "I'm afraid they cannot enter the valley."

"What?" Anand cried incredulously. "But that isn't fair! I answered correctly, didn't I? Wasn't—"

The man in the center, who seemed to be the leader, raised his hand to interrupt Anand's indignant words.

"You misunderstand. You answered well, and thus the gate has opened for you. But there are reasons why we cannot allow your companions in. Abhaydatta—yes, it is he in the mongoose form—has unfortunately spent too much time in an animal shape. It is beyond our powers to transform him back again, even if we are able to counter the poison. We are not allowed to let into the valley someone who is no longer of any use to the Brotherhood. And the girl's mind has been contaminated by Surabhanu. We doubt that we can cleanse it sufficiently to restore it to its original state. A seed of evil may be buried somewhere in it. It may manifest itself years from now in the most destructive of ways. We cannot risk the safety of the entire Brotherhood for her sake."

"But do not worry," the man on the left said, his voice kind, as though he could sense the turmoil raging in Anand's heart. "We will make sure they are taken down safely to the village, where people will look after them. Nisha will be placed with a good family, and Abhaydatta, if he survives, will live with her as a beloved pet. Neither of them will remember the conch, or Surabhanu, or anything else that might trouble them. It is the best that we can do. Believe me when I say they will be content."

Anand frowned. The man's voice was persuasive, and what he said made sense, but something still bothered him. "You mean they'll no longer know who they were?" he asked. "That doesn't seem right."

"Ah, Anand, don't waste any more time," the Healer in the center said impatiently. "We have many plans for you. You have natural talents beyond what we have ever seen. Even untrained, you achieved a rapport with the conch that we would not have thought possible. If you become one of us, you could be the greatest of the Healers the Brotherhood has known, one whose name will be passed down in legend."

"The greatest of the Brotherhood!" breathed Anand. To spend the rest of his life in this beautiful valley with the Healers, learning to develop his special powers and using them to help the world! To be near the conch always and feel that connection, that stream of joy and love that poured from it! He couldn't imagine anything he wanted more.

He seemed to hear faint echoes in his head. They came from long ago.

I want to stay with you and help you more than anything I've ever wanted in my life.

Why, that was himself.

An older, raspy voice answered. *More than anything? I*

think that, perhaps, you don't know yourself as well as you might, child.

Was Abhaydatta right? Did he really not know himself, and what he truly wanted?

"You must not delay any longer," the man on the left said. "It is time for the gate to close." As he spoke, a vibration that seemed to come from deep within the earth caused the ground to tremble. Anand could see the edges of the gateway beginning to move toward each other very slowly.

He glanced back at his companions, still and flat on the ground. They seemed to have shrunk somehow, as though they had receded from him already. He would miss them, he thought sadly. They had shared something special, had been bound together by their common goal and their common enemy. No one else would ever understand how that had felt, no matter how hard Anand tried to explain it.

The doorway was narrower now. Behind it, the healers stood silently, watching him with impassive faces. But Anand could feel their impatience. The conch still lay on the stone where he had placed it, and he thought he felt rays of impatience shooting out from it, too. He tried to quicken his steps as he walked toward them, but his feet felt like they were made of stone. And his heart, too. This was the moment he had been looking forward to ever since he started on his journey. Why, then, was he not happier?

I've done everything I could for Abhaydatta and Nisha, he

told himself, but as he thought them, the words turned into a question. *Haven't I? Haven't I?* And then, like a wave of freezing water, the answer crashed over him.

He stopped.

"What is it, Anand?" the man on the right asked.

"I'm not going with you," Anand said. A part of his mind screamed at him for being a fool, for giving up the opportunity of a lifetime. *What will happen to you now?* it cried. But he swallowed down his fear and went on. "I can't abandon my companions. Send me back to the village with them. They'll need me more than ever, when they wake in a strange place, not remembering."

"But what can you do for them?" one of the Healers asked.

"I'll tell them the story of our quest, and the great sacrifices they made to save the conch. I'll tell them again and again who they were. And even if they never regain their memories, at least I'll have tried."

"But what of your great talent, wasted?" the Healer on the left asked. "Once you learn to use your powers, you could help many more, not just these two."

The Healer in the center added, "You do realize, do you not, that if you refuse us now, you can never come to the valley again?"

Anand nodded miserably. "But if I turn my back on my friends now, what good will I be to anyone? Those virtues we talked about earlier—honesty, loyalty, compassion—

I'll have lost all of them, and without them, my powers can't be used for the right causes. They'll be twisted into evil until I become a creature like—like Surabhanu."

And with that, he turned his back on the Healers and walked to his unconscious companions. He longed to look at the conch one last time, but he was afraid that if he did so, his resolve would weaken, and he would be unable to leave it. *Good-bye*, he called to it in his mind, but he heard no reply. Perhaps it refused to speak to him because it was angered by his choice. More likely that, once he had done his job and brought it back, it didn't care, for to a thing of such immense power, what did the life of one insignificant human matter?

He bent and picked up the still, slight body of the mongoose and sat down next to Nisha. "Whatever happens to you two, that's what I choose for myself," he whispered as he squeezed her cold, seemingly lifeless hand. "If you have to suffer, then I'll suffer with you. I wouldn't have it otherwise, not for all the magic in the world. We are members of the same company, after all." He settled himself down on the snow beside them, shivering. There was nothing to do now except wait.

಴

Was it a moment that passed, or a day, or a year? Anand wasn't sure. He must have dozed, or maybe the cold had pulled him into a white, cottony unconsciousness. He was awakened by a touch on his shoulder. He turned, expecting perhaps a villager, sent to take them down the mountain. He was surprised to find that it was the Chief Healer—and more surprised to find that he was smiling.

"Truly you have done well, Anand," he said, drawing the boy to his feet. "You have done what we wished for but scarcely dared to expect. You put aside your own desire, strong as it was, and chose the path of righteousness, and you did it with love, without which, sooner or later, all choices turn bitter. You have passed the final, most difficult test, the battle that took place within you. It is a feat greater, even, than your defeat of Surabhanu. With much joy in my heart, I invite you and your companions to enter our beloved valley."

Anand stared at him. For a moment, he couldn't comprehend what he heard. And even when the words sank in, he couldn't quite believe them. Was the quest that began for him on a stormy night in the slums of Kolkata—sweeping him away from all that was familiar—finally over? All their efforts and sacrifices to bring the conch back to its home—had they really succeeded? Was Surabhanu truly gone, his powers dispersed into the thin air of the mountains?

In a daze, he heard the doors rumble open again, wider this time. The Chief Healer was leading him by the hand to the stone step. Anand looked down at the conch. Was it shining more brightly, with a lustrous, pearly glow?

"This is why I didn't say good-bye," he heard it whisper.

"Did you know then, all the time?" he asked. And then, a little hurt, "And you let me worry, not telling me anything?"

"I knew all except what you would finally do, Anand— for you had the freedom to choose either way. But I am happy that you passed the test."

"Can you feel happiness?" Anand asked in surprise. "I thought you had said—"

"I am surprised, too. I have never felt such things before this time. But when I thought you might choose wrong and be sent away, that we would not be together anymore, I was pierced by a pain. I think it is what you call sorrow. Ah, it was terrible. One day you must tell me how humans are able to live with such hurt."

"So you no longer think we're such puny weaklings, eh?" Anand couldn't help saying.

The conch maintained a dignified silence.

The Chief Healer was motioning to Anand to pick up the conch. He did so, and was instantly warmed by the current of energy that shot through his body. He offered it to the Healer, though he longed to hold it close and never let go. The Healer smiled, his eyes twinkling—how could Anand have thought that face stern or impassive? Perhaps he guessed what was in Anand's mind.

"No," he said. "It is your place, as Conch Bearer, to carry the conch into the valley."

At the gateway, a line of young men dressed in yellow

robes were standing with flutes in their hands. All at once, they raised the flutes to their mouths, and music filled the air like the softest breeze. No, there *was* a breeze! The parijat trees were swaying, reaching out with their fragrant branches. Silver flowers fell on the travelers' heads as they made their way down the path toward a building that glowed in the morning light as though it were made of ice.

"Why, it's the great hall!" Anand said in excitement. "Inside is the meditation room with its hundred crystal pillars, and a clear roof through which the stars shine down at night. And the hearth where the fire never goes out is there, and in the center, the shrine for the conch. Abhaydatta described it to me!"

"He did well," the Chief Healer said. "Welcome, Anand!"

IN THE ARBOR OF WATER

Three days had passed since Anand had entered the valley, three wonderful days during which he was allowed to wander at will along its peaceful paths and explore its halls and groves. He was provided with a guide, an apprentice Healer named Govinda, a friendly boy only a few years older than him, who was happy to answer all his questions.

Anand soon learned that the Silver Valley was a self-contained community. Everything the Healers needed—and they needed little, for they lived simple lives—could be found within the mountain walls that hid the community from strangers. Physically, the Brotherhood had little to do with the outside world. They helped it in many hidden ways, but most of their work, based on powers of the mind, could be done from the valley itself. Once in a while, when the winter was particularly severe, a couple of Healers might take food and warm clothing down to the villagers to keep them from starving. Other than that, only when a dire circumstance arose—such as the loss of the conch—would they leave their beloved valley.

"But"—Anand couldn't help voicing a small doubt that pricked at him—"don't you ever get tired of living here all the time? Don't you long for a change, or want to experience something new?"

Govinda looked at him, perplexed. "Why would I want to leave the peace and joy of this valley, and the unconditional love of the Brotherhood—especially when, in our daily labors to help the world, we see constantly how it is weighed down with self-caused miseries? Besides, we don't live only in the Silver Valley. We live here, too, and here." He touched his forehead and his chest. "And the landscapes of the mind and heart are inexhaustible. It is said that even the Chief Healer knows only a fraction of what is in there."

⟡⟡

This morning, Anand had spent several pleasant hours in the orchards, watching a group of Healers and their apprentices as they picked ripe mangoes.

"Mangoes! Here!" he exclaimed. Govinda smiled at his excitement and explained that the weather inside the valley was mild enough to grow all kinds of fruits.

"Can I help the apprentices?" Anand asked. A city child, he'd never had a chance to pick fruit, and it seemed so enjoyable. The Healers and apprentices worked in a seamless rhythm, each seeming to know exactly what the others needed from him. As they filled their baskets with the luscious red fruit, they talked and laughed easily among themselves. Anand longed to be a part of them—of the family of the Brotherhood—and he could feel what Govinda had meant when he had said he would never want to leave the Valley.

For a moment, a memory flickered in his mind: another family, other faces, looking with love and sorrow into his face. But he pushed the memory from him quickly, unwilling to let any shadows intrude upon this valley of laughter and light. *Not now*, he said to himself.

"Can I help?" he asked again.

Govinda smiled but shook his head. "You are our guest, and it would be improper to have a guest labor for us. However, if you become an apprentice, there will be plenty of work for you to do! Over on the other side, we grow vegetables. And that's a lot of work. Because the land here is so fertile, weeds grow really well, too! Or maybe you'll be asked to help in the cotton fields. We grow our own crop, so we can spin it into robes. Or maybe you'll be put with the apprentices who help with the animals. We keep a few yaks for their wool. And of course we have cows. I'll take you this evening to watch them being milked. You can play with the calves—they're just a few months old and full of energy. Of course, you mustn't think that this is all we do. Even the youngest apprentices learn how to use the powers of the elements, while the intermediate ones are taught the more difficult skills of far-seeing and far-hearing. And as for the senior-most apprentices—"

At any other time, Anand would have been fascinated by this information, but right now his mind was bothered by something Govinda had said. "Wait!" he said anxiously. "You said *if* I become an apprentice. I thought I was one already. Didn't Abhaydatta choose me to help him? Do I have to pass more tests?"

"No tests," Govinda reassured him. "You've proven yourself many times over. But I'm not allowed to say any more. One of the Master Healers will speak to you soon. Come, I will take you now to see the tower of the wind watchers. Did I tell you about the wind watchers? They are the Healers trained to detect shifts in the atmosphere that indicate imbalances of good and evil."

But Anand would not be distracted. "That's another thing that seems strange. For three days now you've been taking me all over the valley, but I haven't met any of the Master Healers, not since I crossed the gateway. Where is everyone? And especially, where's Abhaydatta? Why hasn't he sent for me? Why haven't I seen Nisha yet? I want to see them, and the conch, too. Why have the Healers hidden it away from me?"

Govinda fidgeted uncomfortably. "I don't know much, being only an apprentice, and I'm not sure how much of that I should tell you, but I can feel your anxiety, so I'll try to answer and hope that the masters will not be displeased with me. The conch has been kept away from us all, for until it is purified and restored to its shrine, exposure to its power might harm us. The girl is well enough, and her leg has been set. But—because she is a girl—we are faced with a problem. As you may have noticed, this is a Brotherhood. There are no women here. So the Master Healers are faced with the question of what to do with her. They have been locked in council for the last three days, trying to make the right decision. Until they decide, she must wait in one of the outer dwellings." Seeing the look on Anand's face, he added, "And no one must visit her there."

"But that's not fair!" Anand said angrily. "Without Nisha I wouldn't be here today, nor would the conch."

"I know," Govinda said. "That's why the council is taking so long to make its decision. They wish to act fairly and wisely and do what is right for the girl—but also they must do what is best for the Brotherhood."

"Well, surely Abhaydatta will stand up in her favor and explain to the council what a true companion she was, and how she has no home to go back to, no family except for us."

Govinda looked even more uncomfortable. "Abhaydatta has been in no position to explain anything. As the Chief Healer mentioned, he spent too long trapped in his animal shape because he did not have enough magic left after his confrontation with Surabhanu to effect the change."

"Does that mean he's going to remain in that shape forever?" Anand asked anxiously, his heart beating fast. He felt terribly responsible for Abhaydatta's predicament.

"No, not that. For the last three days, the best of our shape-changing Healers have been working with him, chanting and praying and calling upon spells of recovery, and they have managed to change him back into his human form. But he hasn't spoken a word, and it is not clear whether his mind is still the animal mind that he had to take on along with the animal body."

"Oh, no!" Anand cried, distraught. His own worries and irritations suddenly seemed trivial compared to what his friends were facing. "I know I'm not supposed to see Nisha, but can't I go and see Abhaydatta?"

"Sorry. No one is allowed to visit him yet either," Govinda said. "The Healers who are with him must not be distracted by the presence of other energies. I am sure that when it is the right time, the Master Healer will make sure you will be taken to him. Come now, it's time for lunch."

"Please!" Anand pleaded. "Ask the Master Healer for me. Maybe I can help him somehow."

"Very well," Govinda said, though he looked uncertain. "I will ask the Master Healer, though he will probably say no. And now, to lunch! Don't shake your head. You won't be able to help your friends if you're dizzy with hunger. Today it is the turn of the herbalist Healers to produce the day's meals. Not only are they are our best cooks, but they also love to play tricks. Did I tell you about the time they made a curry out of the many-hued mountain mushroom that turned our faces all different colors?"

That night Anand awoke with a start in the half dark, his breath coming fast. In his dream, he had been wandering through an underwater palace, following a voice that begged him for help. But though he searched through many waterlogged corridors and doorways framed by seaweed and coral, he could not find the owner of the voice. Even after waking, he could hear the urgent whisper of the voice calling his name, its sadness indicating that there was only a little time left.

For a moment, he stared at the still shapes around him in confusion, not sure where he was. Then he remembered. He was in the northern sleeping hall, with a group of the newest apprentices. But what had awakened him? It was not yet sunrise, though the palest pink glow warmed the crystal that made up the eastern wall of the sleeping hall.

"Anand!"

Startled, Anand whirled around in the direction of the voice, wondering if in this magical place the worlds of dream and reality melted together. But no, this was a real voice, and it came from the doorway to the hall, which, like all buildings in the Silver Valley, was left open at all times. Peering closely into the darkness, he could see a small figure crouched on the threshold.

Anand made his way to the door as quietly as he could. His heart beat so loudly, he was certain it would wake one of the apprentices, and then there would be trouble. But he managed to navigate his way around the pallets successfully, and when he got to the door he saw that his suspicions were right. It was, indeed, Nisha, though she looked strange and unlike herself, dressed as she was in a yellow tunic and pants just like what all the apprentices wore, though hers were too large for her. He was even more taken aback to see that her hair was cropped close to her head.

She saw his look and smiled proudly, shaking a few leftover, uneven curls. "I cut it off myself, with the fruit knife they'd sent with yesterday's meal. I figured it would help me pass as a boy!"

"Nisha!" Anand whispered, his delight at seeing her battling with his anxiety at the trouble she would get into if she were found out. "I'm so glad you're better now. But you shouldn't be here! Aren't you supposed to wait in the outer buildings until they come to a decision about you?"

Nisha nodded. "And I did, all by myself, for three whole days, which drove me almost insane, not knowing what was happening to you or Dadaji, though I guess I shouldn't be calling him that anymore. And not knowing what was going to happen to me didn't help either. But yesterday the Master Healer asked me to come to the council chamber—probably so the healers could see me for themselves and figure out how dangerous I am! They asked me all kinds of silly questions about where I had lived and who had taken care of me before I met

Abhaydatta—as though I needed taking care of! Then they asked me to wait outside in the hallway until someone could escort me back. That's when I heard two apprentices talking about Da—Abhaydatta. They said he just sits by himself all day in the Arbor of Water and doesn't seem to recognize anyone. What's worse, when someone speaks to him, he doesn't respond. He doesn't seem to know who he is. When I heard that, I knew I had to go and see him."

"I've been wanting to do the same thing!" Anand cried. "I've been waiting to hear from the Master Healer."

"That'll take forever—and then he might end up saying no. I heard the apprentices say that no one's allowed to go near Abhaydatta because it might upset some kind of energy flow they've put around him. So if we really want to see him, we'd better take things into our own hands. Dadaji needs us! I have a feeling that I—all right, we—understand him better than all these bearded old men with solemn faces. I don't care if we get caught and punished—or even thrown out of here. And anyway, without him I'm not sure I even want to stay on here. Do you?"

Anand swallowed. He had loved every bit of the valley he had seen in the past few days—its neat, disciplined life, the unexpected ways in which magic and learning intersected here. The world outside the valley seemed complicated and ugly in contrast, and full of cruel men. Every part of him shrank from the thought of returning to it. But he knew Nisha was right. Without Abhaydatta's gentle, loving presence, something crucial would be lost in the valley, and it would harm others as well as themselves.

"You are right," he said. "We must go to him, even at the risk of being sent away. Perhaps we can't do him any good, but I still feel a great need to see him. But how shall we get to the Arbor of Water? I've never even heard the name before this."

"Not to worry!" Nisha flashed him a grin. "On the way back to the outer buildings I asked my escort, very innocently, about what were some nice places to see, here in the Silver Valley—assuming that they were going to let me out of quarantine one of these days. He rattled off a number of names, and every few minutes I made the right kinds of admiring sounds and asked how to get to that particular spot. And that's how I found out exactly where the Arbor of Water is."

"Well done!" Anand said. "What are we waiting for! Let's go!"

❧

The Arbor of Water was off to one side of the valley, separated from the other dwellings by farmland that gave way to woods. Nisha and Anand walked along a narrow trail that wound its way among bamboo thickets and brambly bushes full of wild berries, luscious and purple. They looked delicious, but the children had too much on their minds to want to taste them. The woods grew thicker as they walked. Leafy branches met over their heads, allowing only a little light through, and the forest floor was full of ferns and mushrooms. It was very quiet, even for the valley. The birds and small animals that were seen everywhere else in the valley were absent here.

"It's a good silence though," Nisha whispered. "Not scary. It's like the woods are breathing—the way you do when you're sitting very still and feeling happy about the world."

Now they could hear the sound of water, though it was hard to decipher the sound. One moment it sounded like the whisper of rain on the feathery leaves of the tamarind tree. Then it sounded like droplets falling into a pool, one at a time. Then it was the gurgling of a brook, then the rush of a river over rocks, then the roar of a waterfall. Mystified, the children hurried down the trail until they came to a gap in the trees, and there they stopped, both at once, and stared.

Later, Anand would think it one of the most beautiful places he had ever seen, though if someone had asked him to describe it, he would have found it difficult to give actual details. He remembered green, many shades of it, in the foliage and in the lush grass that grew thickly through the arbor. Rays of sunshine fell through brown branches, lighting little areas here and there, making the dewdrops on the blades of grass sparkle. There were white flowers, bushes and bushes filled with them, and over to one edge, where the shadows were thicker and the air cooler, a spring bubbled up out of the ground and formed a small pool. Next to the pool sat a man, a shawl the color of dead leaves covering his gaunt frame, his head bent so the children could not see his face. But they knew him at once, and together they hurried to kneel on either side of him.

The man did not look up at their approach. Nor did he turn when Anand called his name. When Nisha put her hand on his, he looked at it, but incuriously, as one might regard a branch of a tree, or a patch of grass. Anand's heart sank, but he leaned forward until his face was close to the old man's.

"Remember us?" he asked. "I'm Anand, and this is Nisha."

The old man did not respond.

"You came to my house in Kolkata on a stormy night and asked me to help you bring the conch back to its home," Anand went on desperately. "We came together all this way—you can't leave us like this now!"

The old man said nothing. He gazed past Anand's head, his eyes vacant. There was a black smudge between his eyebrows, like a marking on an animal.

"Oh Dadaji!" Nisha was crying, and her tears fell on Abhaydatta's arm. "You did so many things for me. You bought me a red sweater, and the best pooris and samosas, at the bus station. And even when you turned into a mongoose, you took care of us and saved our lives."

The old man watched the teardrops wetting his skin for

a few moments. Then he raised his hand in a slow, jerky movement to wipe Nisha's eyes. He shook his head faintly, as though indicating that she should not cry.

Anand's heart leaped. Abhaydatta hadn't spoken, but he *had* responded to something. He racked his brain, trying to think of what they might do to draw him out further.

"Sorry, but I can't help crying," Nisha said, hiccuping a little. "You were the kindest person I'd ever come across. Remember when we were traveling and we pretended that we were your grandchildren? Why, that was the best time of my life. Every night I would lie in bed and fantasize that I was really your granddaughter and that we would be together the rest of our lives. But you don't remember any of it, do you?"

Something flickered in the old man's eye, but he still didn't speak.

A sudden thought struck Anand. "Would you like to hear it, even though you don't remember? Would you like me to tell you the story of our adventures, the way you told us stories when we were traveling together?"

Abhaydatta made an indistinct movement with his hand, a gesture that could have meant a yes or a no, but Anand didn't wait. He plunged into the story, starting from the glass of tea he'd shared with an unknown old man on a windy morning. He described the beauty of the conch, how it had transformed his shack—and his life— when Abhaydatta showed it to him. Though it pained him, he told him how, in spite of that, he had doubted the old man. He went on to describe their misadventure at the train station, how they had almost fallen into Surabhanu's clutches. He spoke of the many small ways in which Abhaydatta had taken care of them once they found him at the bus station. His face burning again with shame, he spoke of the temptation he had faced during the night at the inn, and how he had almost suffocated the Healer with his pillow. The hardest part was describing the night in the cave when, thinking that his mother was outside, he had fallen prey to Surabhanu's tricks and broken the protection Abhaydatta had placed around them. "I disobeyed you," he said in a small voice, "and let Surabhanu into the cave. The worst of it was, you were sleeping—because you trusted me—and so you weren't even ready for a battle. He took you away. By the time I could see past that dreadful wind, you were gone, and I didn't even know if you were alive or dead." His voice broke on the last word, and he couldn't go on.

"But I did not die."

Anand looked up, startled. Had the old man spoken, or had he imagined the words with the force of his wishing? He saw a look of amazed delight on Nisha's face. She seemed to be holding her breath.

"I did not die," the old man said again. His voice was wheezy and rusty, but his words were clear enough. "The force of his hatred sucked me out of myself, and my body

was lost in the whirlwind. He examined me in my naked-
ness, and I was too weak to stop him. And when he saw
that I didn't have that which he lusted after, the conch that
he had stolen away, he transformed himself into a serpent
and started back toward you. My only thought then was to
stand between you and him. With my remaining strength,
I turned myself into that which the serpent has always
hated, his mortal enemy, and thus I came to you again. But
in doing so, I spent all my magic and was no longer able to
transform myself back. I traveled further and further into
the animal body, into the labyrinths of its brain, and did
not know the way back. My name fell from me, and the last
memory of my purpose. I lived there and grew familiar
with the mongoose's way of sight and breath, and wished
only to continue that."

"But you remembered us, you did!" Nisha cried. "You
attacked Surabhanu when he was about to hurt Anand.
And if it weren't for you, I never would have broken away
from his spell."

"Perhaps," Abhaydatta said. "Though how much of
my action was from affection of you and how much the
mongoose's instinctive response at seeing his enemy, no
one will know. At any rate, when the Healers brought me
back into this body, I found no comfort in the human
world, this world we have so complicated and corrupted. I
mourned my loss and refused to take back my name—until
you coaxed me into it with your tale."

Anand smiled. Earlier in his life he would have felt proud, but now his heart was filled only with thankfulness. He said nothing—there was no need for words. He held one of Abhaydatta's hands—Nisha kept jealous possession of the other— and after a while the old man lifted his face to the light like someone who is waking from a long sleep and said, "Come, we will go to the hall now. Meditation hour is long over, and morning's work is done. Soon it will be time for the midday meal, and I for one am ready for it."

The three companions walked back to the eating hall. On the way they spoke little, but they laughed often at small things, at squirrels leaping from branch to branch with nuts stuffed in their bulging cheeks, or jays scolding them for stepping too close to their nest. A person who did not know them would not have guessed how close they had been to the brink of being separated from each other forever.

ANAND'S CHOICE

Anand sat in the back of the crystal hall, waiting excitedly for the ceremony to begin. He craned his neck to catch sight of Nisha, who stood in the center of the hall, dressed in the yellow tunic of a novice apprentice, shifting nervously from foot to foot as she waited for the Chief Healer. From time to time, her eyes searched the assembly—looking for him, he guessed. But he was far in the back, behind the apprentices—apparently, respected guests were ranked lower than even the newest apprentice—and she couldn't see him.

Next to Nisha, in a simple shrine made of crystal, sat the conch, and though Anand could not see it very well from the back, just knowing it was there filled him with contentment. It had been returned to its shrine last night. Only the Master Healers had attended that ceremony, which took place at midnight after all the others had gone to their rest. But already the apprentices were whispering about how, when all the peace chants had been sung and the conch was set down in its shattered shrine, there was a sound like a thunderclap and the shrine was whole again.

"And then," Govinda recounted to Anand, "the Master Healer said, 'Truly now with the destruction of Surabhanu evil has been erased and good restored.' All the healers murmured in agreement—except Abhaydatta. He stared westward, with that black mark like a frown between his eyebrows. When the Master Healer asked him what was wrong, he said, 'The roots of weeds sometimes reach deeper than the gardener thinks.'"

"Why would he say that?" Anand asked. Something about the statement made him uneasy.

Govinda shrugged. "The Master Healers often speak in riddles. Don't worry your head about it. If they want us to know, they'll inform us. But now let me tell you about the shining! They say the shining from the conch was so bright that even the Chief Healer had to turn from it and cover his eyes. The afterglow from it filled the entire hall for hours and spilled out into the night outside and made the moonlight pale in comparison. And anyone who was fortunate enough to see that glow—why, his heart is even now filled with a gladness as deep and sweet as the ocean of milk that the old tales say exists in the sky."

Anand listened avidly, brushing away a twinge of resentment at not having been invited to the ceremony. He was happy for the conch, he told himself, now that it was back safely where it belonged—and happy for Nisha, too.

Just yesterday, when he was at the afternoon meal, Nisha had run over breathlessly to the dining hall and, from the door, signaled that she had something important to tell him. Anand had glanced at the Healer presiding over the meal, worrying that Nisha would get in trouble for venturing into forbidden territory. But the Healer had merely inclined his head, giving Anand permission to leave the long, low table still laden with food.

"What are you doing here?" he'd asked as she grabbed his hand and pulled him to a secluded spot under a lychee tree laden with rosy pink fruit. "Aren't you supposed to stay—?"

"Not anymore!" she interrupted him triumphantly. "The Master Healers have decided that I am to stay! That I can be part of the Brotherhood!" She laughed and added, "At first, when Dada—Master Abhaydatta told me, I couldn't believe it. But I guess he spoke to the council about me. You know that he's been in a meeting with them since he came back from the Arbor yesterday, don't you? He convinced them that I would be an asset to the Brotherhood." She preened herself a little bit, as though to say she knew *that* part of it already. "So now it's a Brother- and Sisterhood!"

"I'm so happy for you," Anand had said, squeezing her hand warmly. It was true. His heart was much lighter now that both his friends were safe. But a little nail of jealousy scratched at his heart, no matter how hard he tried to push it away. Nisha was part of the valley now, but what about him? He was still only a guest, treated with deference but kept at arm's length. He had waited anxiously at the crystal hall all afternoon and evening in the hope that either the Chief Healer or Abhaydatta would inform him that he, too, had been accepted as an apprentice Healer, but neither of them had come by. Even Nisha, busy with the preparations for the initiation ceremony—which involved, among other things, a proper haircut—had not been there to allay his anxieties.

Now, sitting in the hall among the Brotherhood, Anand watched as the Chief Healer and Abhaydatta stood on either side of Nisha, chanting the centuries-old words that welcomed her into their midst. He heard her clear girl's voice rise, unfaltering, in answer. They must have taught her the responses last night. Then she kneeled, and he could not see her anymore, only the clear silver stream of water the Chief Healer poured over her head for purifica tion. The Brotherhood rose to their feet, chanting a beautiful, joyous hymn, but Anand, who did not know the words, stood behind them in silence, feeling lonelier than ever before.

~~∽~~

As soon as the ceremony was over, Anand slipped out of the hall and made his way to his sleeping quarters. He did not have the heart to join in the festivities, and he was in no mood to enjoy any of the special delicacies the cooks had been preparing all day. He knew it would sadden Nisha to see him so despondent, and he didn't want to spoil her special day with his gloom. It was clear to him now that the Brotherhood had decided not to choose him. Otherwise, surely they would have initiated the two of them at the same time. He tried to imagine how life would be for him outside the valley, but his frozen mind was able to picture only a thick, greasy grayness, like dirty dishwater. But why? he kept asking himself. Why don't they want me?

He had scarcely laid himself down in a far corner and pulled a blanket over his head when a panting Govinda burst in.

"Oh, here you are!" he said, sounding harried. "I've been searching for you everywhere. What's wrong? Are you sick?"

Anand shook his head. "I just want to rest."

"Well, I'm afraid rest will have to wait a bit, because Master Abhaydatta wants you to meet him. He's in the Hall of Seeing. Do you know where that is? Are you sure you can find it on your own? All right then, you'd better hurry. I want to get back to the feast before the best sweetmeats are all gone." And with that he sped away before Anand could ask what Abhaydatta might want of him.

Anand stood outside the Hall of Seeing, a small, low hall that seemed to be made of tree branches—only they were not dead brown branches but live, leafy ones that intertwined themselves to form a round structure with only a small door leading inside. The door was open, and Anand peered inside nervously, wondering what he should do. It was dark in there, the way it is under a very large tree on a day dark with monsoon clouds, and he could not see much. He jumped, therefore, when he heard a voice say, "You need not wait at the door like a stranger, child."

He stepped gingerly over the threshold, formed of a flowering vine, and immediately felt as though he had entered an underwater space. The light inside the Hall of Seeing was aquamarine, and the walls—but they were not walls at all! They swirled and shifted like sheets of light. Or was it more like the drifting of fog, the ebbing of waves? He stared at them, fascinated, and only slowly did he become aware of Abhaydatta, sitting cross-legged, facing a wall. Without turning, he gestured at Anand to come and sit by him. Anand did so, and together in silence they watched the play of pearly light for a while.

Then Abhaydatta said, "You are wondering, are you not, why we have not invited you to join the Brotherhood."

His gentle voice was harder to bear than any stern decree, and Anand had to fight to keep in his tears. "It is your choice and your right," he managed to say after a moment, though a wave of hurt threatened to engulf him.

The old man put out a hand to cover Anand's, though he still did not turn to look. "Don't be angry, Anand. It is merely that we cannot choose you until you have made a choice yourself."

"What kind of choice?" Anand blurted out. "And how is it that Nisha didn't have to make it?"

"Nisha has no family," Abhaydatta said in his patient voice. "Even our past-seers could not divine where her people were scattered after she was separated from them. Thus she had no conflicting loyalties. But you—you are different."

As he spoke, the Hall of Seeing grew dark, and the segment of wall in front of them began to change color, turning first green, then blue, then a multitude of hues, orange and yellow and red, as though it were an evening sky. A surge of power, like electricity, shot from Abhaydatta's hand into Anand's. He felt the bones of his fingers tingle. The tingling moved up his arm and into the rest of the body, and as it did so, he noticed that the swirls on the wall were breaking into dots. The dots arranged and rearranged themselves until a scene emerged in front of his eyes.

It was a room, a pretty dining room in a modern city flat. Anand guessed it was in Kolkata because a long time ago, when his family had been together—father, mother, sister, brother—they had lived in a place very like this one. Their house had been near the Gariahat Market, and even as he looked into the room, Anand could hear the bustling noises of the city. Wasn't that a hot-gram seller, crying out his spicy wares? And surely those were the clanging bells of the red trams that ran along tracks that had grown rickety over the years? Cars were honking—probably at the numerous cows who lived off the garbage from the vegetable shops and paid no attention to the irate drivers. Unexpectedly, he was homesick for Kolkata—its crowds, its sweat, its vast, beating heart.

The part of the room he could see into was clean and filled with light, with the walls painted blue and an iridescent sparkle of mosaic tiles on the floor. There was a vase of the white tuberoses that his mother loved on the dining table. The table was set as though for dinner, with matching steel plates and tall, shining steel glasses. As he watched, a pleasant-faced, gray-haired man walked in, pulled out a chair, and sat down. Anand drew in a gasping breath. It was his father, though his hair had been black when Anand had last seen him.

"Is this real, what I'm seeing?" he whispered to Abhaydatta, half afraid that the man in the dining room might hear him, half hoping that he would.

Abhaydatta did not answer.

"Bela," the man called. "It smells so good! What have you cooked for us today?"

"He's calling my mother," Anand whispered.

"You'll see what it is in a minute," a woman he could

not see answered. "Better still, you'll get to eat it— as soon as our Meera decides to join us."

Yes, it was his mother's voice, but with a little laugh in it, sounding younger than he remembered. The voice went deep inside him, sweet, but sharp as an arrow. It hurt to breathe, listening to that voice.

"Meera!" his father called. "Meera! You lazybones! Did you fall asleep before dinner again?"

A pretty girl hurried into the room, her hair tied back in a neat braid that reached down her back. Yes, it was his sister, though she looked very grown-up in a new lavender salwaar-kameez. She smoothed down her tunic carefully as she sat down and said, in a mock-indignant tone, "I was doing homework, I'd have you know. Do you have any idea how much work they give us, now that I'm in class three?"

"Am I seeing the future?" Anand whispered to Abhaydatta. He struggled to remember which grade Meera had been in when his mother had to remove them both from school, but it was too long ago and too far away.

"I do apologize, ma'am," his father said, bowing to her, and they both burst out laughing.

Anand's mother walked in then, carrying a bowl of steaming rice, the grains as white as seed pearls. Hungrily, Anand leaned closer to the screen—but it was her face and not the food he was looking at. She looked so much better than when he had left his home. That anxious, overworked look was gone from her face, and her lips, rosy with lipstick, smiled merrily. But there seemed to be a shadow in her eyes, a sadness. And her face was still thin.

"Meera," she said, "come and help me get the rest of the food." When the dishes were brought in, she uncovered them, and Anand saw that she had cooked chicken, a potato curry, and lentils with spinach and tomatoes. By what cruel coincidence had she fixed all his favorite dishes? As she started serving, Anand noticed that there were four plates on the table. He wondered who else would join them for dinner.

"Spinach dal!" Meera cried. "Brother always loved that—" All of a sudden, her face crumpled.

"It's October fourth today," his mother said in a low voice. Anand realized with surprise—for there were no calendars in the valley, nor any concern with them—that it was his birthday. Why, almost a year had passed since he had left home. Surely he had not spent that much time on the road with Abhaydatta! Where had the time gone?

"I know," his father said, his voice sad. "I remember him, too, and pray for him. But, my dear, you've got to stop hoping, as you do each day, that any moment he might walk in through that door."

His mother's eyes were wet, but there was a stubborn glint in them. "You did that, didn't you? Walked into our little shack one morning? I almost fainted—thought I was seeing a ghost."

"My case was different. I'd had the worst luck, I admit it—or else why would I end up working under that scoundrel of a manager who stole from the building funds and then accused me of it, so that I was thrown into jail? The authorities in Dubai wouldn't even let me send you a letter! At least I was a grown-up! Once I got out of prison, I knew how to get back home. But if only I'd come back a few days earlier!" His father struck the table with his fist helplessly, making the dishes rattle, and Anand could see the harsh lines that ran from the sides of his nose to the corners of his mouth.

"It's my fault," Anand's mother said, wiping at her eyes. "I should never have let him go! But the old man— he seemed so genuine. And he did help our Meera get better."

Anand's father shook his head. "It's hard to know good from bad, isn't it? But it's my fault, too, for not being here to take care of you and the children."

The family sat silent for a while, faces bent over their plates, though no one ate. Finally, with a sob, Meera pushed back her chair and ran from the room.

"It does us no good to keep blaming ourselves," Anand's father told his mother. "My heart is heavy, too— heavier than I can describe to you. But we've done all we can. We've notified the police, put advertisements in all the papers, offered rewards to anyone who might find Anand. We've wept for him for months. But now, we all must go on with our lives."

"You're right," his mother said with a sigh, and made an effort to eat. But after a few minutes of toying with her food, she pushed her plate away. The haunted look in her red-rimmed eyes caught at Anand's heart. He knew that she would not forget him so easily. He put out his hand to touch her face, to assure her that he was fine, that he loved her, and always would. But his fingers came up against the cool, hard surface of the wall. At once, the wall began to shimmer and ripple.

"No!" Anand cried. But the room, and all the people in it, had already disappeared into that swirl of color, and only Abhaydatta sat next to him in the Hall of Seeing.

The boy and the old man sat for a while without words in the echoing silence of the Hall of Seeing. Anand's heart was too sore for him to speak, and after a while he realized that his face was wet with tears. He bent his head to wipe them away surreptitiously on his tunic, but Abhaydatta laid a hand on his shoulder.

"Never be ashamed of weeping for love," the old man said gently. And then, "Do you see now why we could not choose you? It is you who have to choose us. Us, or your family back in Kolkata. And as much as we care for you and need you here with us, we would understand if you wanted to go back to them."

Anand's brain was whirling. What did he really want?

To be here in this beautiful valley that time did not seem to touch, to become one with the Brotherhood and learn to use his magical powers? For powers he had, he knew that already, though he didn't know their precise nature. Every morning he could feel them fluttering beneath the surface of his skin like caged birds, asking to be let out. Or to be at that dining table, surrounded by his loving family, filling that empty chair, and the emptiness in their hearts. To live an ordinary life—but ah, such a sweet one. What would be the right thing for him to do?

"I can't think," he said. "I need some time."

Abhaydatta's eyes were gentle with sympathy. "Take all the time you need, my son," he said. "It is a difficult choice—and perhaps the most important one you will make in your whole life."

Anand walked out of the Hall of Seeing. He wandered through the lovely groves and paths of the valley, but for once he was not aware of their beauty. He passed Healers and apprentices at their daily labors and did not see them, even when they smiled and greeted him. But they were not offended. "He is making his choice," they whispered to each other. And some of them, their eyes misty with memory—for they, too, had had to make a similar choice—added with compassion, "May the Great Power guide him."

Anand walked and walked. Was it an hour or was it a full day? He must have stopped to drink water from one of the pools, and perhaps to pluck a fruit or two from a tree, for otherwise he would have been hungry and parched. But he did not remember any such actions. *What to do?* His mind kept repeating. He did not see where he was going, nor did he have a particular destination in mind. Yet he was not wholly surprised when he found himself, in the gentle gloom of dusk, standing at the entrance to the crystal hall where the conch was kept.

The hall was empty. Even in his dazed state, he realized that this was unusual. The hall had been filled with people ever since the conch had been restored to its shrine, even when assemblies or ceremonies were not taking place. The Healers often sat around the conch, meditating, absorbing energy from it so that they could wield their own powers better. Apprentices often sat near it, too, their gaze filled with wonder and awe—and perhaps a tinge of fear. For, like Anand, they guessed that the conch's power extended far beyond their capacity to imagine such things. But mostly what they felt was love, for the conch inspired love in all of them, just as it had in Anand. This, Anand was forced to admit, bothered him the most. Somehow, deep in an illogical corner of his heart, he had believed the conch was *his*, in the way that something you love fully becomes yours. It filled him with jealousy to have to share the conch —even with the Brotherhood. The conch that he had carried next to his skin, the conch that he had been prepared to die for. Why, these callow, calf-eyed youth had no idea

what he had been through for its sake! And so in his dis-
contentment he had stayed away.

But now, here he was, walking down the hall toward
the shrine, his footsteps echoing in the huge, deserted
room. It wasn't exactly dark—it was never dark here,
because the crystal pillars glittered a little and the crystal
roof let in the light of the stars. But Anand stumbled as he
walked, perhaps more from a heaviness of heart than from
not seeing, and fell to his knees. He stayed crouching for a
moment, wondering miserably what he was doing here.

The hall grew bright. It took him a moment to figure
out where the light, pale like the inside of a seashell, was
coming from.

"So," said the voice he had grown to know so well.
"You finally decided to pay me a visit."

Anand stared. The shrine was shaped like a lotus, petal
upon crystal petal, and at its core lay the conch. White-hot
as the heart of a fire, cool as magnolia petals in moonlight.
His heart threw itself against the cage of his ribs, and he
wondered how he could have been foolish enough to have
stayed away even for a day from that which he had missed
so much.

"It was foolish, I agree," the conch said. "And hurt my
feelings besides."

"Hurt your feelings!" Anand burst out. "Not likely!
Haven't you had hundreds of adoring worshipers crowded
around you day and night? I'm surprised you even remem-

ber who I am."

"Ah, a trifle jealous, are we?" the conch said. Anand could have sworn there was a chuckle in its voice. "And very fatiguing it was, too, all that admiration. I was glad when they all finally left today!"

"Why did they leave?"

"I suggested, telepathically, that the work of the Brotherhood was being neglected. It helped also that Abhaydatta asked them to empty the hall."

"But why?"

"Maybe he knew you'd be coming to me."

"But how? Even I didn't know, until just now."

"He's smart, that one." The smile was back in the conch's voice. "Besides, who else can help you make the right choice?"

Hope flared up in Anand's heart. "Do you really know what I should do?"

"I know," said the conch. "But I'm not allowed to tell you. Remember what I said earlier? There are some things humans need to do by themselves. When they've exhausted all their resources and call on me for help, only then can I use my powers."

"I *am* exhausted," Anand said. "I can't think anymore. My brain feels like it's about to burst."

"That's because you're thinking too much, not trying to feel your way through the problem. That's where I can help you. Lie down and close your eyes—go on, don't be shy. The crystal floor is nice and cool, and not as hard as you might think."

Anand did as the conch told him. The floor was amazingly comfortable, and not hard at all. It seemed to fit itself to the contours of his body. He closed his eyes. In the glow from the conch, the insides of his eyelids were the palest rose pink, and he felt himself falling into that soothing color. It was a strange sensation, unlike anything he had experienced, peaceful but also scary. For he seemed to be dissolving into the glow. His arms were gone, and now parts of his legs. What if he lost all of himself, if nothing was left? With that thought, he felt himself tensing up.

From a distance, or from someplace deep inside him, he could hear the conch say, "Relax! Don't worry so much. But perhaps to ask a human not to worry is like asking a fish not to swim! Breathe deeply now, and answer in your mind the questions I ask."

Anand did as he was told. He could feel his breath swaying inside him like the ocean, lifting and dropping thoughts like strands of kelp. After a while, the strands floated away, and in the silence left behind, he heard the conch ask, "Anand, what do you want most to do?"

I want to help people, to make them happy, he thought.

"That's a mistake right there. You can help all the people you want, but you can't make them happy. Only they themselves can do that."

At least I don't want to cause them unhappiness—especial-

246

ly my family. I don't want to be the reason my mother cries and doesn't eat her food.

"Ah," said the conch. "Wait on that thought for a moment, and move to another question. If you really want to help, where do you think you can help more people? Here, after you develop your gifts, or at home with your family?"

I might be able to help more people here, Anand thought, *but they're not my own people, not in the way my family is. I owe my family more.*

"Another mistake," the conch said with a sigh. "All this talk of *mine* and *not mine*. Never mind. You're still young. But if there was a way for you to help your family from right here—more than you could help them by being there in person . . .?"

But how can that be? Anand asked. *What my mother needs is for me to be there.*

"There is another solution. But just for a moment, move your thought away from your mother. Do you want to stay on here, in the Silver Valley?"

I want it so much, leaving would be like cutting off my right hand. But I can't stay here while my family is so sad over there.

"What if they weren't sad anymore?"

But how can that be? I saw them myself.

"Time erodes all sorrow," the conch said. "But you humans are so impatient. You want a solution right now.

Fortunately, that, too, can be arranged."

How?

"Ask Abhaydatta for help."

What can he do?

"Don't you know what his special powers are?" the conch said impatiently. "I know he told you. Concentrate, for the Great Power's sake!"

Anand focused his mind on that time, so long ago, in his shack when Abhaydatta had spoken of the Brotherhood, how each Master Healer had a special talent. *Mine is . . .*, he had said. *Mine is . . .* But the rest of the words would not return to him.

"More importantly," the conch was saying, "you must ask yourself, will you be happy here?" Its voice grew stern and distant, as though it came from a place far removed from the concerns of mortals. "Will you be happy when you are no longer someone's son, someone's brother? For to be one of the Brotherhood is to give up all other relationships and loves. And what you gain in return is not adequate for everyone."

What will I gain?

"Yourself," the conch said in that distant, impersonal voice. Its light grew dim, signaling the fact that their talk was ending. "But only if you are brave enough to look yourself in the eye. Go now and seek Abhaydatta."

Anand raised himself from the floor slowly, as though he were climbing out of someplace deep. When he was at the door, he thought he heard a whisper.

"And myself. I am yours, Conch Bearer, the way I am no one else's. How could you not know that?"

But it may have been only the pines, rustling in the wishful wind.

❧

He looked for the Healer in many places, trying all the while to recall what his special skill was. Several times he almost remembered, but each time he glimpsed the words at the edge of his mind, they slipped away, taunting him. By the time he got to the Garden of Stones, he was both tired and frustrated.

The Garden of Stones stood at the very northernmost edge of the valley, beyond the outlying huts of the cowherd apprentices whose duty it was to take care of the livestock. It lay beyond the pastures, even, where the cows and yaks of the Brotherhood grazed. Anand had not been there before. Govinda had pointed it out to him, a copse of brambly shrubs, and said that he didn't know exactly what was in there. The place was forbidden to apprentices, and even among the Master Healers, only one or two ever went there. Anand had no reason to suppose that he would find Abhaydatta in such a place and had not intended to visit it. And yet, as he was making his way to the Hall of Seeing—hoping, perhaps, to activate the wall on his own—an overwhelming feeling came to him that he should turn northward. Earlier he would have ignored it as foolish, but the journey to the valley had taught him much. So he stepped from the path onto the meadow and crossed it in the dappled moonlight, and in moonlight came upon the little copse that housed the Garden of Stones.

The stones—there were seven of them, set in a circle—were not particularly remarkable in looks or in size, but Anand couldn't move his eyes away from them. They shone white in the moonlight, the color of frozen milk, of crushed opals, and as he approached them, they seemed to grow. Or was it he who was shrinking? The air around them rippled, a mist drifted across Anand's face, and it was as though he were in a different place, in a different age, a windswept moor with the stones now towering above him. They pulsed with a power that drew him nearer. A chant in a language he did not know was rising and falling all around, as it had done—but how did he know this?—for centuries. He put out his hand to touch the stone closest to him, knowing that once he did so, something important would change. He wasn't sure if the change would occur in his life or in the larger world, or if it would be a good change or an unfortunate one—and right then he didn't care.

A hand caught his shoulder, holding him back. "No, Anand, it is not for you to touch the stones," Abhaydatta's voice said.

Startled, Anand turned. How was it that he had not seen the old man? Abhaydatta was wrapped, as usual, in his cotton shawl, which shone as white as the stones in the moonlight. Or had he not been there until now? Anand shook his head dazedly. There were too many mysteries to this valley! He'd have to ask Abhaydatta about it later. Right now he had a more pressing question.

"Why must I not touch them?"

"They are the stones of memory," Abhaydatta said, "sent to us many centuries ago from the other side of the Black Waters. Only Healers who possess certain powers may approach them. If others touch them—well, the stones would absorb their memories and leave them with no past."

All at once, the words he had been trying so hard to recall struck Anand in the face like a salt-spray wave. "You are a master of remembrance and forgetting!" he exclaimed.

Abhaydatta gave a little bow. "That I am, among other things," he said, and smiled.

"Is that why the conch said you could help me? It said you could make sure my family wouldn't suffer if I decide to stay here."

"Yes. I have the power to make them forget that you were ever a part of their lives. But are you sure that is what you want? For once done, such a thing cannot be undone."

Anand's mouth was dry. To say yes would mean shutting the door to his past forever. To become a person without family, alone as a leaf snatched by a gale. To be unremembered—was it not a kind of death? He closed his eyes tight and thought of his mother's face, the look on it when she would wake him early in the morning in their dim Kolkata shack so he could go to his job at Haru's tea stall. Concern and regret and love, all mixed together. No one would look at him quite that way again. Could he bear to give it up, even for the conch?

"Can you make me forget, too?" he asked.

"No." There was sorrow in the Healer's voice, but also firmness. "Those of the Brotherhood must remember, no matter how much the pain. They must remember all that they sacrificed for the sake of becoming a Healer, for only then will they value what they learn here. With every step they take into their new lives, they must realize that—"

Anand heard his own voice completing the old man's sentence. "—in order to gain something great, one must release his hold on something else equally beloved."

As he spoke the words, he realized that he had made his choice.

HOME

Dressed in the same old shirt and pants that he had worn when he entered the Silver Valley, Anand stood in the center of the crystal hall, staring at the crowd that filled the great space all around him. Everyone who lived in the Silver Valley must be here today, he thought, and shivered a little with nervousness. It seemed as though he had been standing here for hours, waiting for the Chief Healer and Abhaydatta to approach him. His pants were stiff with dried mud, and his shirt smelled and made his skin itch. Its green color, faded though it was, still appeared too garish in the sea of pure white that surrounded him. He wondered once again why the clothes, which had been waiting for him at the foot of his pallet when he woke this morning, had not been washed. He stared at the crowd again, fidgeting, feeling dreadfully out of place in his city attire. All around him, there was a throbbing in the air—the conch's power, enormous, unfathomable, but kept in check, like the fire breath of a sleeping dragon. Was it wise to place so much love on an entity you didn't understand? Anand thought, and the thought made him suddenly afraid.

Then he caught sight of Nisha, sitting among the new apprentices in the back. She waved wildly and gave him an irrepressible grin. The Healer to whom she had been assigned frowned at her and shook his head. But it made Anand feel a little better to know that she was out there, cheering for him—even if she didn't fully understand what he was going through.

✧

Last night, after making his decision, he had asked Abhaydatta if he they might go once more to the Hall of Seeing.

"Yes, indeed," Abhaydatta had said. "In fact, I would have invited you to come, if you had not already request-ed it." He had smiled at Anand, and the very sweetness of that smile had made it impossible for Anand to stop the tears he'd been trying to hold back. Abhaydatta had put an arm around his shaking shoulders.

"Weeping is not bad," he said. "It clears out the heart, making space in it for growth."

They walked in silence to the Hall of Seeing.

"You must wait for a little while," Abhaydatta said, "while I do my work. I will call you when all is ready."

Anand sat on the cool wooden steps outside the hall, watching the fireflies flit through the dark. He felt a great sadness, in spite of all of Abhaydatta's consolations, and more than a little guilt.

Am I making the right choice? He wondered again, and heard again in his mind what the old man had said in reply.

If you stayed with us, it would be the right choice. If you went to your family, that, too, would be right.

When the moon had traveled halfway across the sky, Abhaydatta came to the door of the hall and called him in. Together, they sat, hands linked, in front of the wall, which shimmered and changed. They saw in front of them a scene similar to what they had seen earlier. Anand's father sat at the dinner table, teasing Meera, who swung her braids and said something pert and funny. His mother came in with platters of food, and laughed to hear them joking. She served them and sat down to eat. That was when Anand noticed that something was different. There were only three places set at the table.

"They don't remember me anymore," he whispered, and satisfaction and sadness coursed through him at the same time.

"That is so," Abhaydatta said.

"It feels like a part of me has died."

"How else will a part of you be born tomorrow?" Abhaydatta said. But he rubbed the back of Anand's hand for a few moments, his wrinkled fingertips so gentle that Anand wondered if he, too, had felt as torn when he had joined the Brotherhood.

"May I watch them for a little while?" Anand asked.

"Watch as long as you want," Abhaydatta said. They both knew, without speaking of it, that this was the last time Anand would see his family.

Anand watched with longing as his family ate and talked of the mundane occurrences of their day. His mother had found some excellent baby eggplants at the vegetable shop. She would fry them whole for dinner tomorrow. Meera had had an arithmetic test at school, and thought she had answered all the questions right. Anand's father was planning a trip for the family to the seashore at Digha in a month's time and had just received the brochures he'd sent away for. As Meera cleared the table, he brought out pictures of guest houses they could rent, and asked his family which one they liked the best. Anand gazed at the three heads bent close over the brightly colored pictures, trying to feel their excitement. At one time, a vacation to the seashore would have been the highlight of his life. How many times had he and Meera daydreamed about such a trip. They would run on the beach all morning, feeling the hot sand between their toes until they plunged into the cool, salty waves. They would eat fresh fried fish for lunch and lounge with books all afternoon, and at night they would stroll with their parents to the bazaar to buy sweet laddus and watch the flame eater performing by the gates of the Amber Palace hotel. But the images no longer charmed him. He would always love his family and their world of simple, daily joys, but it wasn't enough for him. It had shrunk—or had he grown? In either case, he could no longer be held by it.

He closed his eyes tight, as though to capture, forever, the images that floated in front of him. Then he let go of Abhaydatta's hand and watched the walls turn dark.

Now, standing in the middle of the crystal hall, he felt regret again, but it was very faint, like the call of a bird from the other side of a lake. It was mostly excitement that surged through him now as his eyes caught a movement at the door. Yes, Abhaydatta and the Chief Healer had appeared and were walking toward him. As they came closer he saw that the Chief Healer carried a pitcher of water, just as he had for Nisha, but in Abhaydatta's hands there was a bundle.

When they stood on either side of him, he saw that their faces were solemn, as the ceremony dictated, but their eyes shone.

"We welcome you into the Brotherhood," the Chief Healer said, his voice ringing out over the hall. "You brought us back our hope and our power. Indeed, you brought back the life of the valley, and we thank you for that. Now you have chosen to give up much to be with us, and we appreciate that, too. It is my hope that you will find among your brother—and sister—Healers a family equally loving as the one you left, and a home equally secure.

May you learn much and heal many, and do your part to keep the valley safe, and the world also."

Anand kneeled, and felt the cool water washing his hair like rain. A few drops wet his lips, and when he licked them, the taste in his mouth was one of sweetness. Abhaydatta was raising him up now. He felt weightless, as though he might float away. He guessed that this was the end of the ceremony—that was how it had been with Nisha—and that people would come up and congratulate him now. So he was surprised to hear the Chief Healer speak again.

"Amongst all of us in the Brotherhood who have been blessed with gifts, you have a unique one. We meditate on the conch and draw our strength from it, but you have spoken to it. And, more importantly, it has spoken back to you."

A murmur of surprise rose through the hall, growing into excited whisperings. The Chief Healer raised his hand for silence.

"I therefore welcome you not only as our newest brother, Anand, but as the new Keeper of the Conch."

Ecstatic applause broke out around Anand as he stood dazed and flushed. Keeper of the Conch? Even in his wildest fantasies he hadn't dreamed that such a thing might happen. He, Anand, the butt of Haru the tea-stall owner's gibes and jokes, the boy whom the rich, school-going children laughed at as an ignorant lout? He was going to be the person who took care of the conch for all his life?

"Abhaydatta, to whom you are apprenticed, will explain your duties to you," the Chief Healer was saying. Fingers were unbuttoning his dirty shirt, letting it fall away. From the bundle he carried, Abhaydatta took out a long yellow tunic like the ones all new apprentices wore. It was only as he slipped it on that Anand realized it was different. It had a tiny conch embroidered in yellow silk thread over his chest. As he stepped out of his old pants, he ran his fingers over the smooth pattern and could not stop smiling. He wanted to turn to the conch in its shrine, to say something about how happy he was. But everyone was talking to him at once, holding his hands in theirs, clapping him on the shoulder, welcoming him. A small figure threw itself at him, almost knocking him over. It was Nisha, her eyes shining.

"This is so great!" she said. "I'm so proud of you." And then, in typical Nisha fashion, "Just don't get a big head now, okay?"

Over her head, Abhaydatta's eyes twinkled at him. "I'll see you after the noontime meal in my cottage," he said. "There is much for you to learn and no time to waste. Don't be late!"

"I won't!" Anand said. Be late! How could Abhaydatta think he might be late? Didn't he know how long Anand had been waiting and hoping for this moment, for the chance to study again? And not just ordinary subjects! He would be studying the magical arts, the ones that would open up a whole new universe to him, one that he had seen only in tantalizing glimpses. He couldn't think of a better teacher to work with! And at the earliest opportunity, he was going to ask Abhaydatta what he had meant when he told the Chief Healer "the roots of weeds sometimes reach deeper than the gardener thinks."

The bell rang, indicating that it was time for the noon-time meal. "I'd better go," Nisha said. "I'm supposed to sit with my Master Healer and his other apprentices, but I'll come and see you and Dada—I mean Master Abhaydatta, as soon as I can." She ran off with a wave. Others filed out of the hall more decorously, and Anand started to follow them.

"Wait a minute," a voice said behind him, dryly. "Aren't you forgetting something?"

Anand whirled around. "I wanted to talk to you, but there were so many people around—"

"Excuses, excuses!" said the conch grumpily, but from the silver glow that radiated from it, Anand guessed that it was only pretending to be upset.

"I can't believe I'm supposed to be taking care of you," he began excitedly.

"Actually, it's the other way around, but you humans, you always like to think you're in control. The Keeper before you, he got it into his head that he had to give me a bath every month. He would actually put me in a bowl of soapy water and scrub me with a toothbrush. Can you imagine the indignity! Don't you be getting any such ideas now."

"If it's my job to scrub you," Anand said sternly, "then scrub you I will. And no whining about it."

The conch gave a disgusted sigh.

Then Anand said, a little shyly, "Does this mean I'm allowed to touch you?"

"Of course, dimwit! You're the Keeper, after all."

"May I touch you now?"

"You may," the conch said loftily.

"How will I get to you? You're shut up inside the crystal shrine."

"Sorry, can't help you with that one," said the conch. "Remember the rule?"

"Yes, yes, I know," Anand said. "If I can figure it out myself by using my human intellect, then you aren't allowed to tell me. Who made that rule anyway?" His voice grew suspicious. "It wasn't you, was it?"

The conch gave a haughty sniff. "Now you want to know all my secrets? Next you'll be asking me who the candy seller in the train was, and the blind beggar woman!"

Anand examined the walls of the oval shrine carefully. There were no doors or hinges that he could see. How was he going to open it? A little nervously, not sure he should be doing this, he put out his hand to touch its cool surface.

But there was no surface to touch! He watched in amazement as his hand went through the curve of the crystal all the way to the elbow, feeling nothing. He watched his fingers pick up the conch and bring it out through the walls.

"Can everyone do this?" he asked.

"Hardly! Try it with your other hand now."

Holding the conch carefully to his chest, Anand reached for the shrine with his other hand. But this time, he couldn't even reach the oval. A powerful force pushed his hand back from the crystal shrine, and when he tried to force his way through it, pain nipped at his fingertips as though he had touched a live wire. He jumped back with a cry and glared accusingly at the conch.

"Well, you did want to know, didn't you?" the conch said. "I made the shock very mild, actually. It's usually many times stronger."

Anand shook his head to clear it. He was startled by the fact that the conch had hurt him. He'd have to ask Abhaydatta about that, and about how all this was done— more questions in the long list of queries he had for the Master Healer. But meanwhile, he held the conch close, and forgot the pain he had experienced. Instead, he felt awe flooding his entire body, just as it had in the dim hovel in Kolkata when he had first seen the conch. He thought, again, that he had never come across anything as beautiful.

No, *beautiful* was too small a word to contain the conch. His heart swelled with gratitude.

"You're not so bad yourself," the conch said.

Anand grinned as he replaced the conch, marveling again at how his hand slid through the crystal as though it were water. But then he remembered a question that had been nagging at him for a long time. "Can I ask you something? Couldn't you have stopped Surabhanu when he was stealing you? Didn't you have enough power for that?"

"Could have fried him into a crisped potato."

"Why didn't you, then?"

The conch was silent for a while. "I'm not sure I can explain it in human words," it said finally in that distant, impersonal voice that always troubled Anand. "It's complicated. You see, everything's connected in the universe. It's something like a giant spiderweb, except the webbing is made of the most beautiful material, like threads of light that sing. Sometimes bad things—or things that seem bad—have to happen so that wrongs elsewhere can be righted or other good things come to pass. Sometimes an action is set in motion, and it must be allowed to run its course. To stop it forcibly would wrench the design of the web. The Brotherhood was growing lax and complacent. That is how a person like Surabhanu was able to enter the Silver Valley in the first place. The Healers had to lose what they held most valuable before they could learn to appreciate it—and their gifts—again." It paused. When it spoke again, it was in a lighter tone. "And if I had stopped Surabhanu, how would you have come into the valley? You, and that wild girl you've brought along with you. She's going to shake up the Brotherhood, you mark my words."

"But your Keeper—he died for you."

"Ah, death!" The conch gave a sigh. "You humans are always making such a hullabaloo about death. His body was old and tired—it was time for him to crack that mold and emerge from it, to take on a higher form. He knew this as he was going, and was not sorry—and nor was I—for he died performing his duty."

Anand stared at the conch. It saw death so differently and spoke of it so casually. He wasn't sure he could ever feel this way about death—his or another being's. He wondered if, when it was his time to die, the conch would be so matter-of-fact about it.

The conch must have sensed Anand's thoughts, for it said, "Now don't you fret! You're going to be around in that scrawny body for a long time! You have a lot of learning to do before you're ready to take on a higher form! And speaking of time, there goes the final bell-call for the noon meal. You'd better run. Today's meal was prepared by the Healers who take care of the cattle, and they make the best milk-sweets ever."

Anand's stomach growled. He realized, all of a sudden,

how famished he was. "See you tomorrow!" he called over his shoulder as he hurried toward the door.

"And the tomorrow after, and the one after that," he heard the conch say inside his head as he ran toward the dining hall down a path edged with sweet-smelling mint and fennel, herbs that ease the heart. "There's work to do. Strange things are stirring out in the world, and we must watch for them and keep ourselves ready. But we'll do it together, Anand, you and I, Abhaydatta, and Nisha. We're the Company of the Conch, still and always—and don't you forget it!"